EX PARTE

episodes of existential fiction

SHELI ELLSWORTH

BeachHouse Books

Saint Charles Missouri   USA

www.beachhousebooks.com

BeachHouse Books

Saint Charles Missouri   USA

an imprint of

Science & Humanities Press

Author's Note

Remember, there are three simple truths about religion: Jews don't recognize Jesus as the Son of God, Protestants don't recognize the Pope as the Vicar of Christ and Baptists don't recognize each other at the liquor store.

Contents

Lynchburg Correctional, 1845 1

Lunch Date 12

Fly Away 16

Last Dive 19

Under the Pier 24

The Parting 30

Last Dance 35

On the Edge 42

The Gift 45

Going Perfectly Straight 47

The Trick 52

Double Stuf Oreos 54

The Bee List 61

Eureka 70

The Ticket 82

Lipstick Chronicles 90

Mittens, Mama and Mashed Potatoes 103

Summer Psychology 108

Fortune in the Fountain 112

Drought 118

Legend of the Blue Morphos 121

First Day…First Grade 127

Gambling on Motherhood 130

The Exhumation 134

Scattered Ashes 140

The Roadmaster 151

Lynchburg Correctional, 1845

The vilest deeds like poison weeds, bloom well in prison-air;
it is only what is good in man that wastes and withers there;
Pale anguish keeps the heavy gate, and the warder is despair.

Oscar Wilde

Warder Logue—05 June 1845. Today, I assume the position of warden. 'Tis a hot, sultry Virginia summer. The men stink and the place is dismal. Rat droppings are everywhere and the food smells deplorable. I, myself, would go mad under the circumstances of this filth. The hangman's noose would seem a welcome reprieve. I will begin reviewing the prison files tomorrow.

Personal Ledger—08 June 1845. My staff is amenable and tries to make me comfortable, but I miss my Elizabeth's attentions and fussing. I hate being so far away; leaving her in Boston was a difficult choice. Even if she could have come, I cannot imagine asking a wife to these conditions. A stale breath hangs in the air. The grime on the floor is enough to make one retch. Elizabeth would have ordered me to commence boiling buckets of water. The bill for the lye alone would have bankrupted the place.

Warder Logue—10 June 1845. I am amazed at the strength of these men. The human need for survival is a remarkable mechanism. There have been outbreaks of every sort. The infirmary seems to have treated over a hundred instances of small pox, ague and cholera this year. The lack of beds and sanitary practices must be the cause.

Warder Logue—11 June 1845. Most of the men have been convicted of blatant offenses, a den of thieves and murderers, some less guilty than others, mine is not to judge though. And young, some of them are so young—I, myself was skipping rocks and climbing trees.

Personal Ledger—12 June 1845. Elizabeth weighs on my heart. Her soft breath against my neck seems long ago. I ached for her embrace at the doorway of our small, cozy cottage. The smells of simmering pots and her gentle touch beckoned each dawn and called me back each eve. The strength a man has in his work is dependent on the strength of his matrimony.

Warder Logue—15 June 1845. We are to receive twenty prisoners from a unit in Alabama—closed due to rioting. The conditions were rumored to be so malignant, it was reported the men were picking larvae from their barley mush and their slop buckets overflowed. I must begin to walk the corridors and meet these roughnecks I am in charge of. Their names and files can only bring part of their stories. Faces. I need to see the faces of evil.

Personal Ledger—15 June 1845. I think if any of these men had the good fortune to share their lives with an honest woman, we could have reduced their numbers by half. 'Tis the family men strive for, not drinking and debauchery. I can only hope the fairer half of humanity does not give up on the rest of us. Chaos would surely ensue. I would have gone mad without the distraction of sanity my dear Elizabeth has provided. I cannot imagine being locked in a cell where I could not feel her tenderness. I must make plans to go to back.

Warder Logue—17 June 1845. A local pig farmer has offered to supply us with fatback at a fair price. If I move the new men to the West Ward and close down the smaller one, I can afford to purchase it. Maybe they would not mind the crowding if the mess situation improved. The cook that prepares my food makes a fine dish, but 'tis not something I can enjoy. The food turns to swill in my mouth knowing my prisoners are eating slop, and I am reminded of how much I miss my dear wife's cooking. Decent food alone can soothe a man's soul.

Warder Logue—21 June 1845. The improved rations may have calmed some of the unrest since the Alabama men arrived. I made the trip through the corridor today without incident. Yesterday, someone spat as I tried to inspect the wing housing the new men. A 5 x 7 space is too small for two men. I must make the other ward operational. One of the youngest men looked at me with such fear—I need to look into his offenses. He is thin, but of muscular build. His lack of beard and tow head tell me he is a mere boy, too fair to survive with hardened men.

Personal Ledger—29 June 1845. I cannot wait to return to Boston and escape this stifling heat. The dead air has brought a malaise that might be relief to the guards, but signals trouble to the rest of the staff. Men who are ripe for fits of consumption and nervous breakdowns, madness the most dreaded of all prison endemics, no way to quarantine the sick or isolate the well.

Warder Logue—30 June 1845. I examined the frightened boy's records. Jonathan William Speaks was convicted of horse thievery. His statement says, "I just come upon the mare eatin' grass next to my papa's fence. Twern't no brand. I was just keepin' her till her owner showed. Didn't 'tend to hide her from her rightful keeper." The judge, however, claimed that holding her in the barn was nothing but plain guilt. A boy of fourteen years does not belong in this hole.

Office of the Warden—01 July 1845. According to Mr. Greer, my assistant, the prison has been without a chaplain or priest for over a year. Like all prisons, we have cases of donated Bibles that usually end up in the storerooms serving as dens for the rodents to breed since most of the men are illiterate. The Catholics have no one to hear confessions, the Protestants have no one to baptize…do not the evil still have souls? Surely, I am not expected to intern men's spirits also? I will call on the local parishes and see if I can find clergy mad enough to join the rest of us on occasion.

Personal Ledger—05 July 1845. *God knows I could use a better mattress. My predecessor Warden Oliver, his predecessor [and their wives] and probably their predecessors shared the rutted hole I am wallowing in each night. I am quite certain I will find myself on the ropes soon. However, the men sleep on string hammocks the rats have gnawed. Any one of them would give a right arm for my discomfort. My bed in Boston, while not a king's loft, was bathed in Elizabeth's sweet scent making for an imperial sleep.*

Warder Logue—13 July 1845. This morning, I strode the corridors and saw the boy again. His cellmate, Samuel Carson, is of middle age and convicted of murdering his younger brother. A history of thieving and robbery, the two of them. Just a matter of time until one of them went down. The Carson brother looked square at me with cold, obsidian eyes—a place no soul could breathe. I am afraid for the boy. I asked Mr. Greer to have him moved to solitary. "This ain't a racehorse stable, Sir. These here are rats and weasels. They belong caged together," he told me.

"He's just a boy," I said. "Neither rat nor weasel." I looked up from my paper. Greer is not a man known for his Christian nature. He is stout, cut from rawhide and stone. Does his job well, scheduling guards and overseeing visitation, but I would not want to see him angry.

"Where would ya have me put 'em, Sir? I ain't got no single right now. Thief or murderer be the only choice."

"Put him with someone younger," I told him, "a more inexperienced thief or murderer. He's too fair to be in with the Carson brother."

"Aye. He is a pretty one. Prettier than my sweet Sally. . . there ain't no safe place, Sir."

"I'll be opening the other wing soon. Keep him safe until then."

4

"Yes, Sir. Do me best."

Personal Ledger—14 July 1845. *I dreamt of the Speaks boy last night—when I pulled my own son's small body from the drowning water and turned him over, the face was that of Speaks.*

Warder Logue—15 July 1845. I called on three ministers and a priest this afternoon. The priest is considering assigning me his younger charge who reminds me of a robust St. Francis. Of the three ministers, the only one that might be willing to visit is also the youngest. Youthful naivety seems to be a defining gradient. I can recall my own tender ignorance before I knew of the squalor inside here.

Personal Ledger—15 July 1845. *My dear Elizabeth, I miss you so. There is a boy in prison here, a mere lad of fourteen. He reminds me of the son we lost—an innocent gone to poor judgment and freak circumstance. I am worried for his safety. This is a place for ironclad criminals, not a boy who failed to find a horse's owner. I must find a way to help him. I see the way the men look onto him.*

Warder Logue—16 July 1845. I am having the prisoners scald and scrub the ward. In the newer prisons, the men have no labor. They are to be silent and alone; each cell is solitary. The newest ones have plumbing in every hole. Even the White House has no such amenity. Quakers are spearheading the new prison design. They are certain that goodness is in the nature of all men; that prisoners only need quiet reflection to find it. I fear the nature of man is not so clean cut.

Personal Ledger—16 July 1845. *This morning, Greer and I were walking the grounds. I asked him if he found a safer cell for the boy.*

"Sir, I can assure you that Master Speaks is safe 'cept from himself," Greer said.

"And what provisions have been made for his security?" I said, taking longer strides than Greer could muster.

"I have moved him to the old storage room. It has everything he needs and more Bibles than he can possibly read."

"Surely you have not locked the boy away with rats in the dark!"

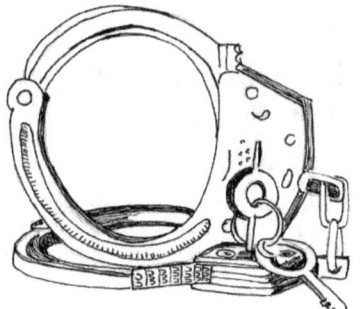

"Sir, 'twas the only option. While I've many keys, I am not an innkeeper."

This was only one of the galling conversations I had with Greer today. Upon arrival at the point where the properties meet, I shared with him my thoughts to plant the lower acreage in the spring. The idea of growing some of our own food and using the cornhusks to make mattresses for the men was not well received.

"A blight on the community, Sir—the men in their prison stripes working the dirt. Another reminder that a prison sits right on the edge of a sleepy hollow of God-fearin' families."

"The men need better food and something to do. Most of them men got into trouble because they lack skills. This will bring them opportunity. A man must have a plight to rack."

"Sir, these are not men. They are what be left after the soul leaves the body."

"Mr. Greer, I have not been sent here to judge these prisoners. That has already happened. I am here to manage this institution. I will not starve, torture or enslave these men. All work will be voluntary. Those who work will enjoy the fruits of their labors, as it were." Fortunately, for me, the sky opened, releasing a much promised rain, and Greer and I ran for the cover of the building.

Warder Logue—29 July 1845. The young priest, Father O'Connor, came for the first time today. He was clearly stricken by what he saw. He wishes to begin Catholic services on Friday eve. Greer sends the day guards home at five. The service must be

6

over before they leave. I could have the men's dinner served earlier, but it is too long afore breakfast. Surely, a riot would erupt.

Personal Ledger—04 August 1845. Father O'Connor and I have much in common. We are both from Boston and enjoy a good cigar. I am still concerned about the boy. He has been moved to the infirmary due to rat bites and is not the first prisoner to have suffered such fate. I do not know if he was bitten in his sleep or tried to make a pet of one. 'Twas my fault he was in the storage den, but Greer is not a man to be taken lightly. He lives by a code of conduct descended from barbarians, hardened by his duties, worsened by his lack of height. He is tough beyond measure.

Warder Logue—09 August 1845. We opened the small ward today. Prisoners must be shackled, guarded and hooded during transfers. Some prisons use the hoods and shackles with much frequency. The shackles serve little purpose in a single cell and the hoods even less. However, for the transport of prisoners, they have proven valuable.

Personal Ledger—13 August 1845. Sweet Elizabeth, I miss you so. I may have approached a way to liberate young Master Speaks. I am desperate to relocate him as our infirmary has reported his release back to general population tomorrow. In the morning, I will confide in the only one I can trust here—Father O'Connor. I will pray for forgiveness and that he not think I am mad.

Warder Logue—14 August 1845. I visited Father O'Connor this morning early. We have worked out arrangements for an earlier service. The men will be pleased.

Personal Ledger—14 August 1845. I told Father O'Connor about the Speaks boy and he was quite shaken. A flat look dulled his face as if a dire portent had been spoken. His eyes clouded over with a film of tragedy. "A boy so young," he said, almost silently. "'Tis sinful." He touched my shoulder with a hesitant hand—a man who had known pain. "I too was once accused of something I didn't do," he said. "I left Boston when a widowed parishioner accused me of impropriety. The poor woman...so mad from grief, I think she succumbed to lunacy."

"Then you understand," I told him. "Father, I must free this boy from what will surely be his demise. I see how the men eye him, hankering for his youthful innocence. I know I am considered a man of honor, trusted to maintain the integrity of Lynchburg. I was sent to this position because I can be counted on to do the right thing, but Father what is the right thing? I would surely never sleep again if I left this boy to his fate in prison."

"What, if anything, can you do?" His blue eyes started intently at my face.

"I could help him escape," I said, swallowing hard.

"It would be too dangerous to bribe the guards. One would surely tell," he warned, shaking his head. I sensed he had already come to peace with the crime I was going to commit.

"Not bribe them, but fool them."

"Are your guards given orders about escaping prisoners?"

"Yes, they have permission to shoot."

"So, your plan involves violence?"

"I suppose it might. But keeping the boy locked up will surely lead to violence or worse."

"Ah. A difficult choice. You should ask the boy."

"Father, I need your help. The guards would not harm you or watch you too closely."

He looked into my eyes calmly and without reservation. "What would you have me do?"

"A note. Could you give him a note?"

"Can he read?"

"His file says he was in school through the fifth year," I said.

"Even the poorest student should read by then. Give me the note. I will try."

Warder Logue—16 August 1845. Today was our first Catholic service in quite some time. I was impressed so many men, including Protestants, chose to attend. The men were orderly and no extra guards were needed.

Personal Ledger—16 August 1845. *I can only hope the boy received the note and understands the message. I must wait a week to see if he accepts the Father's next one.*

Office of the Warden—16 August 1845. Mr. Greer has asked me about the Alabama men's transfer back to Huntsville. He bore a telegraph that said that only a portion of them would be leaving. I have since instructed the telegraph office to deliver all messages directly to me. Greer's curiosity is not to be taken lightly.

Personal Ledger—23 August 1845. *I think I may have convinced the boy to cooperate. I will visit the Father tomorrow and go to the telegraph office. I have booked a ticket to Boston for September. My tenure from Elizabeth has been much too long.*

Warder Logue—24 August 1845. I ordered all of the men's heads shaved. An outbreak of lice has jeopardized the Alabama men's transfer.

Personal Ledger—24 August 1845. *It occurs to me, when all of the men are shorn, they are strikingly similar. Father O'Connor has agreed to accompany the men on the first leg of their journey. The men trust him and the guards will not question his presence. He has notified the monks at the Spencer Abbey, asking acceptance for Master Speaks, and to provide him with asylum until he is older. Arrangements for his travel will be made.*

Warder Logue—24 August 1845. I have received word that sixteen of the Alabama men will be leaving on Friday evening by riverboat. My guards will escort them as far as Greensborough where they will travel by rail to Huntsville.

Warder Logue—30 August 1845. The Alabama men will be leaving after Mass this evening. Four guards have been assigned travel duty. Hoods and shackles will be worn until the men are given over to the Huntsville guards in Greensborough. The James is at a lull now; their boat ride should be an easy one. I sent the riverboat man a barrel of ale as gratuity. He loves the drink, I am told.

Personal Ledger—30 August 1845. *I dare not breathe until my guards have returned safely. I stood at the door of the vestry when the men were pulled aside for the transfer. I held my senses still, while the captain of the guards shackled them together.*

Warder Logue—12 September 1845. I have received word that the men were safely delivered. The guards and Father O'Connor are on the return trip and should arrive by Friday.

Personal Ledger—17 September 1845. *Father O'Connor arrived early for his Mass liturgy and came to my office today. He pulled my door to and leaned his baldpate over my desk. His voice quiet—almost a whisper—he told a most remarkable tale.*

"We all boarded the boat. The men had problems with the small gangway since they could not see. They finally settled down once the guards loosened the chains. The boatman was more than willing to offer the guards some drink after the prisoners had fallen asleep. I promised to keep watch over them while the guards and the captain played cards and drank.

"After the moon had been out for some time and the guards were taken in by the card game, I shook the boy awake and unshackled him with the extra key you gave me, taking care not to rattle the chains. The fright on his face bore upon me, while I gave him my extra clothes and put the stripes on myself in case of a count. Then I put my robes over a bag of tobacco we were hauling, laid down next to the men, and pulled the hood over my head. I told the boy to hide and then ease himself and the loose shackles overboard as soon as the guards became loud and swim to the east shore and wait for someone from the Abbey. I, myself, was trembling by this moment…after several hours, the guards had dozed off and I went into the bunkroom with my robe around me and changed the besotted captain's transport orders for the ones you gave me. The movement of the boat and the sound of the river hid my presence—tho I feared my cantered breathing would wake

10

them. I hid the old orders in my clothes, then found my bunk and pretended to sleep. One of the drunken guards walked the boat, a few moments later, but did not awaken anyone or sound the alarm.

"When I finally got up, the guards had removed the hoods for the morning meal and I could hear some discussion about the men. I held my breath while the captain found the transport orders, counted the men, and then things seemed to settle down."

His eyes widened when he asked if there were any reports of missing prisoners. I said, 'No,' and sensed his relief."

Personal Ledger—25 September 1845. *Hotel Williams, Boston. I bought a great handful of flowers, early this cool morning, for my Elizabeth. Seeing her and our son was a comfort to my soul. The pasture has grown over their graves. The still of the cemetery soothed my fraying spirit. I have missed them so.*

Lunch Date

Carol passed away a month ago. We spent fifty-two years together. Seven grandchildren and thirteen great grandchildren, her obituary said. Carol had lived a full life, and so had I. Come to think of it, Carol was my life. Her sudden heart attack had left me adrift, stranded in a sea of uncertainty.

No, I didn't want to move out of our home. I didn't want her clothes donated to Goodwill. I wanted her back. I wanted the smell of cinnamon in the kitchen, disinfectant in the bathroom, and perfume on the sheets. I wanted flowers in the yard and soup on the stove. I wanted to be able to turn a tasteless, frozen pizza into a meal.

Men never plan on living longer than their wives. We're just not geared that way. We take for granted that toothpaste appears from the cabinet, clothes go from being dirty and wrinkled to fresh and smooth, as if by magic. We are empire builders, financial wizards, and handy men—if nagged enough. We are not keepers of the hearth or capable of remembering birthdays. We cannot maintain life-saving first aid items in our purse or note pads and doohickeys in our pockets. We're no good alone. We require the gentle pressure of honey-do lists and bills delivered in envelopes with our name on the front. We need to be reminded to buy toilet paper and dental floss—things we never think about until we need them.

When Carol passed, I was not only a man without a compass; I had no idea where the compasses were kept. My wife was the organizer, the inventory supervisor.

Last April, just weeks after her passing, I'd been reading the paper trying to decide what to do for lunch. I had eaten at McDonald's the day before, Mexican from down the street the prior evening. What about the new place on Carlson Avenue next to CVS? No, I'd already had lunch there—nothing to write home about.

I stood at the cluttered kitchen table that had become my work station since Carol's death. *What's in the freezer?* Walking across the kitchen, I opened the door and inhaled a whiff of old ice and Italian sausage. A lone pizza sat on the top shelf. It wouldn't kill me. Not if I remembered to take the cardboard off the bottom or start a fire—like last time. I preheated the oven, remembering to push start. I finished reading the newspaper, waiting for the remnants of the previous cheese fire to waft out the stove's vent. As I unwrapped the pizza and placed it in the oven, the doorbell rang.

Peering through the peephole, I saw an unfamiliar face and a covered dish. I pried the door from its snug resting place and smiled at a woman about Carol's age.

"Hello," I said.

"I hope I'm not late," the round-faced woman said, pushing her way past me. "The traffic was just awful. I'm Nancy, by the way."

Shuffling to the side, I wondered aloud, "Late?"

"You know, every time we do this, someone gets lost, but today it isn't me." She smiled, heading toward the kitchen.

I'd always made myself scarce while Carol's writing club members discussed their latest efforts.

Suddenly, the doorbell rang again. A taller woman who looked vaguely familiar was standing there holding two potholders pressed precariously on the ends of a casserole dish whose glass lid was collecting steam and threatening to blow.

"It's been so long since we've met at Carol's. I got lost. Fortunately, I saw Nancy's car and then saw her on the porch. I'm Celia."

"Come in Celia," I said. Celia walked toward the kitchen as if guided by a knowing hand.

Why are these ladies from Carol's writing group here? They'd sent condolences when she passed. Hadn't they? I was a little behind on my email. Had I missed something? Carol was always so good about keeping up with computer stuff. I figured if anyone needed to get hold of me—well, the phone still works.

As I attempted to sort through the question of unanswered correspondence, the doorbell's Westminster chord chimed again. This time three ladies stood there, impatient for me to step aside. I smiled. Carol always said it was my best feature. I surrendered the entryway to the smell of perfume, hair spray and…cardboard! Again! I'd forgotten about the damn cardboard!

I rushed ahead of my visitors and threw open the door to the gas chamber door that had incinerated the last pizza.

"No worries," one of the women said. "We have enough for everyone."

Within minutes, the women were setting the table, pouring ice tea and fishing napkins from the pantry, which held little else. Before I could object, explain or ask forgiveness, we were all seated at the table and my plate was being filled with smoked salmon, egg salad, broccoli salad, fruit salad, kale salad…maybe this was a salad club? I didn't recall Carol belonging to a salad club.

"Where is Carol?" someone asked.

"She had a dental appointment this morning," Nancy said.

Oh no! They think Carol is still alive. And we were having such a wonderful lunch, too! I really hated to spoil it…maybe after

14

another serving of potato salad or dessert…I think I saw a cake pan.

I waited. Yes, it was wrong. But who was I to ruin these lovely ladies' luncheon?

Finally, after a bite of what the ladies' called a flourless chocolate cake, so exquisite—the only word I feel comfortable using, since I no longer take those little blue pills—I dropped the bomb.

"Ladies, I hate to tell you this, but Carol died."

"Carol Finsky died? Oh my God! I just spoke with her yesterday. Oh my God! What happened?"

"Not Carol Finsky. My wife was Carol Campbell. I'm Irv. Irv Campbell. This is our house."

"Well, Irv, I'm so sorry…but our book club meets at Carol Finsky's. Isn't this her address: 15721 Meridian Way?

"You're close…we're at 15771 Meridian."

"Irv, I'm so, so sorry. Why didn't you stop us?"

"My Carol used to have her writing group over…I thought you might be her friends."

"Irv, when did your Carol die?"

"About a month ago."

Nancy pushed herself away from the table. "I better call Carol's—the other Carol—she is probably wondering what happened."

"You can invite her over," I volunteered. And that's how I became a bona fide member of the Westlake Ladies Literary Society. Lunch is at my house in September.

Fly Away

A baby robin was lying near the sidewalk on the brisk spring morning. It was naked and pink with narrow slits for eyes. I couldn't help myself—without thinking, I lifted him carefully from the grassy grave. His skin was wrinkled, fragile. He bobbed a tiny head when I held him. I looked in the elm overhead and glimpsed a cradled nest about halfway up the tree.

There was a time when I would've returned the fledgling to his home of origin. A time when I would've thought he'd fallen out and needed to go back to the safety of his mother's care. But experience and natural selection had taught me that his mother probably pushed him out of the nest. Not because it was time for him to be on his own, but because she sensed that something was wrong with him, and the food she provided for him was probably wasted. He would never make it in the wild. The extra nourishment could go to siblings that had more promise, a greater chance of survival and the chance of having offspring of their own.

My own mother hated imperfection. She was tall and thin, a talented, beautiful, and intelligent brunette. Just the sight of me as a newborn must have caused her to cringe—red hair that stuck straight out, a foot that rotated inward.

But human mothers don't abandon deformed offspring. Human mothers love and nurture. They believe that all children have potential.

I decided to carry the baby bird home and at least see it through its final hours. I found an old fuzzy sock and made a small nest. I placed the bird in a shoebox hoping to make it feel safe.

I never felt safe. Both of my parents suffered from depression. There were constant highs and lows, ashtrays full of foul cigarette butts, and beds that were rarely made, because the depressed need their escapes. My mother thought she could berate, criticize and somehow mold me into the perfect child she deserved. I wasn't allowed outside because my skin was too fair. I could never wear pink, or lime or red because I just "didn't have the coloring for it," she would say. I was never allowed second helpings because I was already big enough.

I decided to get an eyedropper and try to give the baby bird some water. I was surprised at how thirsty he seemed. He swallowed several drops and then rested his head on the edge of the makeshift nest. He was stronger than he looked.

Mother was convinced that I would never do anything right. I could never be good enough: My choice of crayon colors was wrong; I failed to hold my pencil properly, my posture was inferior to her own. As a teenager, she hated the way I wore my hair. As an adult, the hospital corners on my bed sheets were never tight enough.

Inspired by the bird's progress, I decided to dilute a tiny bit of commercial cat food and see if he would eat. He chomped on the eyedropper with his delicate beak, taking several gulps. I thought I could see his eyes opening a little more. He seemed grateful and once again situated himself where his head rested on the edge of the curled sock.

Somehow, I survived my childhood, in spite of belt marks and their incisions to my self-worth. Out in the world, I found myself drawn to what I'd known as a child. There were boyfriends who put me down and bosses I'd never please. I married, longing for relief; for words that did not lacerate and hopes that weren't dashed against the harsh reality of my own limitations—a few safe moments away from criticism and pain. It wasn't long before that too was gone. I finally fled physical and emotional abuse and landed hard, alone and without anything except the echo of my mother's voice telling me she told me so.

But unlike the baby bird, my wings took flight. I flew away from depression and criticism. I soared above the belittling and carving of my soul. I made a nest of my own, one that celebrated uniqueness.

The baby bird is not moving much. I see shallow breaths and faint heart beats through thin skin as he struggles. He is so tiny and helpless. I notice that one of his wings is smaller than the other. I admire his determination. I sit with him while he makes peace with a life that he never asked for. An hour later, he ceases to move. He is gone. I want to cry for him, for his defiant struggle.

Last Dive

It was one of my earliest memories—deep aqua blue water, humidity, and chlorine that burned my nose and stung my eyes. I wasn't very old: a child of four or five. My sitter, whom I called "Nanna," took us to the local university's indoor swimming pool at least once a week. There were two of us younger ones and her older son.

The building itself was the only one on campus with a dark river-stone façade. Its interior acoustics echoed sounds off the painted cinder block walls and cement deck. I loved the warm water, especially in winter when ghostly steam hovered above. Being with Nanna and her son Steve was the only time I felt part of a real family. I called Steve, "Tee," and considered him an older brother. My own parents were busy—no time to hang out at swimming pools or parks. But Nanna didn't mind loading us up in her bulky blue Buick. She seemed to enjoy the outings as much as we did.

Tee was almost a decade older than I was, practically grown by my standards. He seemed so confident. At the pool, he tossed his towel on the bleachers the minute we arrived and headed for the tallest diving board. Tee would dive off the boards over and over. I'd watch him go in the water, then resurface minutes later somewhere I never predicted.

I, on the other hand, had to stay in the confines of the shallow end. Sometimes when I was feeling brave, I'd grab the spillover-ledge and inch my way into the deeper end of the shallow-half of the pool. I felt brave only until my arms became tired, and I realized that my feet could no longer touch the bottom. Then I would slowly inch back to the safer depths.

But I wanted to be a big kid. I wanted to jump off the diving board that looked a hundred feet high. I wanted the freedom of walking to the other end of the pool by myself. I wanted Tee to look at me as an equal and watch me dive into the water and swim like he did. Maybe what I wanted was my independence, or maybe I just wanted to change my status from being *supervised* to being *super*. It's not easy being trapped in the body of a four-year-old. Even if you had to act mature—no temper fits, no complaining about food on your plate—everyone still considered you a little kid. I wanted to run wild around the block, climb trees, knock on doors—ask if some kid could come out and play and watch cartoons at the neighbors without asking permission.

Sometimes Tee would sit and watch television with me, and sometimes we ate sweet, dry Cap'n Crunch out of a bowl. I loved to color with Crayolas in my coloring book. Once, Tee surprised me by coloring with me. He used bold colors: reds and blues. He pushed firmly on the crayons, creating a texture with them I'd never seen before. I admired his masterful technique as the sweet, waxy smell filled the space between us.

He'd even been known to launch an exciting game of hide-n-seek. He could hide in places I never imagined. It was as if his extra height gave him knowledge of a world of which I could only dream. He could reach for a glass in the cabinet and get his own drink of water. He could walk over to his friend's house by himself. He could tie his own shoes and ride a bike. I wanted the same. I longed to leave the house without my parents' permission, to eat food straight out of the refrigerator.

The next summer, Tee rode his bike to the swimming pool on his own. He was on a swim team. Sometimes Nanna would take me to watch the team train. I couldn't wait for my legs to grow and for my arms to be long enough to hoist myself out of the pool without using a ladder or steps. I wanted to swim to the deep end and make the kick turns that would catapult me toward the next end. I needed to tread water and to hold my breath without panicking. There was a lot to learn to become a big kid. And the longer I waited, the further ahead Tee would be. He would never see me as a friend or equal until I could swim the length of the pool or do a back flip off the edge.

By the next summer, Tee had abandoned me for complete independence. He rode all over town and rode on a bus to compete in swim meets. I rarely saw him. Sometimes Nanna would take me to watch, but he never spoke to me at those events. He was with his friends, a clique to which I'd never belong.

After that summer, I was too old for a sitter, and I hardly saw Tee. I heard my parents say that he was smoking cigarettes and hanging out with some kids who smoked pot. I didn't believe it, people love gossip—spice to the batter of everyday boredom.

The old pool in the university's stone building was closed when a newer Olympic-sized pool was constructed not far away. The new pool had an underwater observation deck, skylights and three diving boards instead of two. I took swim lessons there in the summer. It was so large that several lifeguards were always on duty.

Sometimes I thought I saw Steve there, but he never spoke to me. Even once, when I made eye contact as he walked by, he didn't respond. Maybe he didn't remember me. Tall, handsome, maybe he was too cool to know a red-headed kid half his size and I was too shy to ask. One summer I thought I saw him with a whistle and dressed in black lifeguard shorts. If it was Steve, he was never on duty when I was at the pool.

Finally, I was a high school senior, training in the dead of winter hoping to make the university's swim team. Even though there was snow on the ground, I forced myself to swim countless laps every day.

Tryouts for the coming fall were in the spring and included a mile swim, I was committed to the pool for a least an hour every dark February evening and I was not alone, at least two dozen others also dared the sub-zero temperatures. The long workouts were arduous. For someone swimming indoors in a heated pool, I still considered training a monumental effort. After the mile of laps, I'd loiter in the shallow, waiting to catch my breath and hoping no one would notice my enervation.

One Thursday evening, I watched the divers and noticed that many of them would stay underwater after their dive then surface at the wall opposite the diving board where I was resting. One diver looked familiar, but he was so far away I couldn't tell who he was. He went into the water…I never saw him surface. But the pool was so large; I could've easily missed him.

Fifteen minutes later, a fellow lap swimmer came up.

"Hey," he said, also mentioning that there was someone on the bottom of the pool. He got out, walked over, and told the lifeguard. I saw her shake her head and smile. No one seemed concerned. The lap swimmer came back and said the lifeguard reported there were underwater divers training in the water. His face looked tight, and his eyes squinted. Then he dove back in toward the deeper water. Moments later, I saw another person speaking with the lifeguard and pointing intently to the pool's blue murky water.

The next thing I was aware of, the lap swimmer was pulling someone toward the shallow end. The lifeguard ran over, and they laid him on the deck and immediately started CPR. Another lifeguard called 911 and came running to help. The body was lobster red. They turned him over and tried to empty his lungs using another position. Water from his mouth and nose streamed away from the scene toward the drain on the deck. Everyone got out of the pool and stared while paramedics began their desperate fight. As they were lifting him on the stretcher, I caught a glimpse of a swollen face. It looked like Tee.

Maybe I was wrong. Maybe the rescue efforts and the excitement had clouded my judgment. Surely it wasn't Steve. He was an excellent swimmer and more at home in the water than anyone I'd ever known. But it looked like Steve. Older, but still tall and handsome, even after the resuscitation efforts; thick hair that curled when wet. The kid who was never afraid of anything. The kid who could hide on top of a grape arbor, climb a telephone pole, and eat Cap'n Crunch without milk…

Under the Pier

It's dawn. The streetlights have ceased their eerie glow. Since daylight savings stopped, the days are longer. I feel safer. I sleep better lying down, but here on my cement Posturepedic, propped up against the rough stucco wall next to a FedEx drop box, I can see anyone approaching. I usually steal a couple of hours of sleep in the early morning, but sleeping on the sidewalk takes a wretched toll on my back and neck. I wake up unable to move, and the pain sears my head. Sometimes I rent a cheap room with another loose shirt, usually at the beginning of the month or around the 15th, and get a good night sleep and a shower. People are more generous around payday.

How many times had I walked or driven by a homeless person without worry? How many times did I think about giving them a couple of bucks but stopped because I didn't have much cash or figured I shouldn't encourage begging and the lifestyle it propitiated? A lifestyle? This isn't a lifestyle. It's just waiting for things to get better—waiting for my ship to come in.

Harold stirs on the other side of the metal drop box. Harold is probably in his sixties but looks older with missing teeth and sunken cheeks. He is pretty harmless. Harold would rather sleep with a bottle of Wild Turkey than a woman. I'm safe with him, although the pungency of whiskey and clothes that cry for a match light can be stifling.

I stand up, stuff my blanket into my backpack and walk toward the liquor store. If I'm careful, I can urinate in the bushes behind the building without detection. Not having a real restroom is difficult. When I was living out of my car, I could drive to places with public facilities and clean up. Now, sometimes I walk to the mall and use their restroom to wash up. Stores get suspicious if they see you more than once. They start asking questions and shoo you away. Harold buys his hooch at the liquor store, so they let him use the bathroom there.

When I return, I see Harold's secondhand sneaker tunnel out from worn dark chinos. "Hey, Harold. How ya doing?"

"Aw, I'm good. I guess. It wasn't too cold, so I got some sleep."

"I'm gonna walk down to the mall today. You wanna come?"

"Naw. I'm gonna go to the river and clean up, then down to the pier."

"Okay." I pull out a Rice Krispy Treat for breakfast. I'd found a box of them behind the grocery store last night. Wally's keeps the dumpsters locked except when they toss stuff on the midnight shift. Once I found a bakery cake: red velvet with white icing and sprinkles. There was a tiny bit of mold on one edge of the piped icing, but for the most part, it was perfect. The sweet vanilla smell reminded me of cakes I used to buy before I lost my job, beautiful three-layer cakes with cherries and chocolate curls for birthdays. I shared the moldy cake with Harold because, well, I can't carry a whole cake around all day and stashing stuff has its own problems: bugs, risk of theft and the lingering mold.

When I was in nursing school, we studied molds and fungi in microbiology. They're categorized as opportunistic pathogens, saprotrophs, and thermophiles. Funny I can still recall that. Penicillin revolutionized medicine and it comes from the mold *Penicillium chrysogenum*. Lovastatin, a cholesterol medication, is also derived from a mold. *Tolypocladium inflatum* spawns the immunosuppressant drug cyclosporine. I still can't eat moldy food though. Expired food, food thrown out by restaurants and delis, but not mold.

The mall doesn't open until ten o'clock, but I like to get there early right after the restrooms have been cleaned. It keeps me from picking up viruses and worrying about being sick without insurance or money for cold medicines and the like. I try not to look in the mirrors, though. It's better if I don't see my reflection. I used to always wear mascara and lipstick. People said I was pretty. But living on the street, I'm better off looking unkempt. It's safer. My street friend Sophie always put on lipstick. Sophie was raped and when she reported it, they took her away. I haven't seen her since.

I finish the Rice Krispy Treat and bid Harold a *salut,* since he used to teach high school French. It is early enough that I can walk slowly, normally. Usually I walk fast, like someone who is just getting her morning exercise because I'm less likely to be recognized and pitied by people who knew me when I was a nurse.

It's ironic that the whole house of cards started to teeter when I was treating a homeless woman in the emergency room. It was three a.m. and she came in with a sore throat and sores in her mouth and nose. I was bending and squatting, looking for enough samples for a complete round of antifungals when my back went out. I finished my shift, went home, took an NSAID and went to bed. The next morning I could barely roll out of bed. I used ice packs, took more anti-inflammatories, but was no better when I had to go to work three hours later. I had some Vicodin left over

26

from a dental problem. I took a couple of those and they got me moving just enough to go to work.

I tolerated the pain for a week with the help of the Vicodin and the NSAIDS. Finally, I got Dr. Mecham, the ER doc, to give me a prescription for muscle relaxers. They seemed to help, but when I took them with the Vicodin I was virtually pain-free. When I ran out of Vicodin, I asked the resident orthopedic surgeon to X-ray my back. He came up with a diagnosis of degenerative disc disease. I could've diagnosed that myself, but he gave me a prescription for another hydrocodone. It kept the pain in check for over a year, but every month I had to increase the dosage. And I did feel better. I felt so much better, I was able to work double shifts in the ER. I even started to do my own yard work.

Then I began to run out of the medicine before the prescription expired. I talked the inexperienced night pharmacist into refilling it once or twice, but the doctors told me I needed to see a pain management specialist and stopped giving me scripts. I bought a script from one of my ER patients. By the time I had it filled—without insurance—it was almost $300. What was worse, the medicine I needed was within my reach. I had access to drugs that relieved my pain and I was handing them out to people with sprained ankles and bad hips. People who could go home and use ice and bed rest to relieve their pain while I had to be on my feet for twelve hours at a time.

So, I started to pocket a pill here and a pill there—just enough to keep me going, because now the rebound effects of the pain were increasing. I could hardly move without the meds. And the more I tried to cutback, the more depressed I became. I figure it was a function of the pain and withdrawal. Whatever it was, my brain stopped functioning at its normal capacity. I began to make mistakes. I was late to work. I tried to dispense NSAIDS instead of hydrocodone to my patients and keep the pain meds for myself, but a hospital is not a place where people suffer in silence. I found myself dispensing more pain meds than normal and some of the doctors became suspicious. After a while, I was asked to leave. As soon as I had to start buying the pain medication on the street, I couldn't afford to live in my house. I slept at sympathetic friends' homes for a few weeks. But when I started to run out of money, it became more difficult to get out of bed and do anything more than look for vikes. I lived out of my car for quite a while without anyone knowing how bad it was. Then my car was impounded after I'd left it in a tow-away zone because I had to give some sleazebag more than money for a script. It was probably for the best anyway. My registration was about to expire.

But this morning is beautiful. Walking to the mall, I realize how wonderful this area is. I couldn't live on the street in New York. The cold weather combined with my back problem would be deadly. Sometimes after I clean up and fill my water bottles, I ask people in the mall parking lot for money. If I can get five dollars, I'm good. If I can't get any money, I'll scavenge for plastics and aluminum cans. It'll take all day, but today I have the Rice Krispy Treats, so I'll make it. Maybe I'll just go look for Harold and hang out at the beach. In some ways, I feel lucky. My kids are grown. I'd hate to be alone, pregnant and homeless. Now I just worry about myself. I don't worry about mortgages, insurance payments or giving to charity. I worry about today. I worry about my next meal. And if I'm having a bad day, I just go down under the pier and sleep it off.

My back still bothers me, but I'm not on the pills anymore. Sometimes, I just have to be alone and cry it out. The tears remind me that I am still a human being. I'm still a person, even though I don't get a paycheck and people usually look away when they realize I am homeless. Then I think about how happy I was when my children were babies. I tried to be a good mother and wife. I didn't worry about pain or meds. I worried about Easter baskets and tooth brushing. I worried about not being too critical and buying shoes with good arches. I cooked broccoli and made flashcards. I tucked my children into bed and then, exhausted, I pulled my own covers up. Later, when they were in high school, I went to nursing school and made flashcards for myself. Then I graduated and sent my children to college.

I have much to be thankful for. I did for my children what my parents couldn't do for me…my dad was an alcoholic. It was a good day when he drank so much he passed out.

Maybe I'll call my daughter next week. It's her birthday. I don't want her to know where I am or why my cell phone is disconnected. She has babies of her own. She needs to worry about them, not me.

I think Harold has the right idea. I'm going to go to the beach instead of the mall. Once or twice, I sneaked into the hotel on the water and washed my clothes while I laid out on the sand. Then I figured out it was cheaper to buy things at a thrift store than put coins in a machine. And sometimes thrift stores throw good stuff away…. Another reason to go to the beach hotel is that sometimes people who get room service leave leftovers outside the doors. So, if I'm really careful, I might slip in and see if someone's Eggs Benedict betrayed them and found its way to the hall.

But I do love the beach. The steady sweep of the waves is almost womblike and the smell of salt is welcome refreshment. Sometimes people abandon their beach umbrellas and I claim them for my own, staying under them as long as I like. Under an umbrella, I don't feel homeless. I have a roof over my head. I could be anyone. I could be a rich lady from Beverly Hills who just comes there because she loves the sound of the ocean. I could be a nurse on her day off enjoying the breeze and the surf. I could be anyone at the beach.

I have a lot to be thankful for.

The Parting

I heard a noise outside my bedroom window. A rustling, then
scratching on my screen. I moved toward the interruption and
raised the blinds, unlocked the window and lifted it as far as my
nine-year-old arms would allow.

"They're here! They came this morning. Come on . . ."

"Now? Let me get dressed. See you in a minute." It was all
I could muster so early on a Saturday. I traded my cat pajamas for
jeans and a t-shirt and grabbed a Pop-Tart before seeking out my
flip-flops. My mom was still asleep, so I closed the screen door
slowly and without its usual slam.

I headed down the hill behind my house where Tad and I
had found a common preoccupation with the small stream that cut
through the back of our neighborhood. There was an old utility
building perched on the bank that had become the neighborhood
hangout. But this morning was different. Tad and I would be the
first and only ones to witness the arrival of our new visitors.

My feet slid on the sandals that cut between my toes as I
made my way toward the gray structure. Rounding the corner, I
could see Tad standing on the concrete step in shorts and a
Spiderman t-shirt. I'd known him long enough to predict what he
would say in the next five minutes: "They're awesome! You've
never seen anything like this!"

30

I slowed my pace as he bent down further on the step. "Be careful! They're little. Aren't they awesome? Look at them…hundreds…have you ever seen anything like this?"

And they were everywhere. The culmination of weeks of speculation had now paid off and Tad's predictions had come true. Baby praying mantises were crawling all over the ground, seeking what—I did not know. They were amazing—clumsy and elegant all at the same time. New and green, they headed for the grass and weeds nearby. Safety maybe. An instinct perhaps.

Tad and I knew about safety. It was how we learned to survive. The stream had become a safe place that was ours. Away from yelling mothers and drinking fathers. We had found each other and a way to avoid the harsh realities of life in the dirty factory town.

"Gotta go. Today we get new shoes," he said.

"The Flyers? Are you getting the Flyers?"

Tad looked at the new insects one last time. "I don't know. I doubt it. Maybe."

Tad's mom had three kids—that's six feet and thirty toes. Tennis shoes were probably a big deal, but since Tad's mom was like mine, I knew that anything which required putting a cigarette out was even a bigger deal.

I stayed with the mantis siblings and ate my Pop-Tart. I envied them. No one telling them what to wear or what to eat. No one criticizing their hair or their unmade bed. "They only live about a year," Tad had told me. A year was probably long enough, I thought. But at the time, I was only eight, and a year seemed pretty long.

I trudged back up the hill. Without Tad's blond hair and blue eyes, the mantis excitement had died. I'd known him for most of my life and wished I could see the world through his eyes. Everything was more interesting when we were together.

No one was awake when I snuck back into the house. I braced for the quiet to be interrupted by the slamming of doors or the ringing of phones. Creeping back into my room, I decided to go back to bed and savor the morning's solitude and wait for Tad to come back.

I heard the car pull into the next door drive. Gravel from the road made small pops as it hit the driveway's pavement. I looked out the window and heard Tad's mom yell for everyone to grab a bag as she stood next to the car. I wanted to throw open the front door, speed toward the shoppers, investigate the new tennis shoes and ask stupid questions just so I could see my best friend, but a voice inside of me said that I was already dorky enough and running across my yard to interrogate him about something over which he had little control was pretty ridiculous. I would wait. And I did.

I didn't see Tad for several hours—Saturday cartoons were the best. I couldn't compete with Batman or Scooby Doo, but I could clean my room and do my chores just in case I had an afternoon invitation. An hour into my task I heard scratching on the screen and I again repeated the ritual.

"Hey, let's go down to the water."

"Sure. Let me ask my mom. Where's your new shoes?"

"At home. Mom won't let me wear them to play in."

"What did you get?"

"Um, just some tennis shoes."

"But what kind?"

"I don't know…they're blue."

Hedging…he was avoiding my question. Why wasn't he telling me? Were they really ugly? Were they girl shoes? "I'll be down in a minute." I shut the window.

I arrived at the stream in time to see Tad stretch out his leg and reach one of the bigger rocks that occupied the water's edge. "So, how was the shopping?"

"Okay, I guess."

"Where'd you go?"

"Loehmann's"

"Really?" My mom said they were overpriced. She took us to Sears. They gave factory employees a discount.

"Yeah. My mom wants us to dress better. We're going to be moving...a new school and stuff . . ."

I didn't know what to say...moving...my best friend...my only friend. "What? When are you moving? Why didn't you tell me?"

"I just found out."

"When?" I blurted out again.

"As soon as school is out, I think."

I felt numb. I couldn't imagine him not living next door. Not being there every day of my life. I don't remember much about the last month of school or how much time we spent together. I do recall the moving van pulling up in front of his house. I wished I could pack up the ache in my heart and send it on its way like all of the toys and furniture on the truck next door. I didn't know when the van left. I couldn't bear to see it pull away, but I did notice it was gone about the same time the sun went down.

Then the familiar scratch on my screen. It was Tad, pointing toward my front door. I paced to the doorway wondering what—if anything—he could possibly have to say. I opened the door and there he was in the new blue Flyers.

"I just came to say goodbye."

"Goodbye," I responded.

"I have something for you," he said, pulling a jar from behind his back.

I stared at the lumbering insect, now still, in stubborn denial.

"It's a mantis. Maybe one of the ones we saw as babies. Remember, they don't live very long. You might want to let it go in a little while."

"I remember. Maybe I'll let it go when it gets a little more mature."

And I did.

Last Dance

If you don't know who the crazy person in the room is—it's you.

I think I came to find out if I was nuts. Or I came to find out why he left me. Why *had* I agreed to meet him? The answer is as absurd as our relationship.

"Come on in," Mark says, opening the painted front door. He stands there dressed in jeans and a button down striped shirt that makes him look even taller than his normal six foot height. He is still handsome.

"How are you?" I say, not expecting the truth.

"I'm good. You look great," he says, smiling through thousands of dollars worth of orthodontia and cosmetic veneers.

"I thought you were working out of town. Someone said you were on the San Diego run."

"I still come home every weekend. The San Diego thing is just until I get my pilot's license."

He offers me a seat on what had once been my sofa. A recalcitrant accent pillow slides to the floor. As I reposition it, he offers me a glass of wine. Wine sounded good, but caution prevails. "How about some ice water?"

"The water here just gets worse and worse. This is the only city I know of with piss-flavored water. How 'bout a Coke?"

"Water is fine. I'm used to it." I'd given up cola along with my other teenage transgressions like all-nighters, clove cigarettes, and bad boys. Mark had slithered in through a crack in my psyche

35

formed after adolescence when I realized that my parents had lied to me—I wasn't smart or pretty. I made good grades, but nothing my peers couldn't match and there were plenty of attractive girls my age—most of them tall blondes with tanned legs as long as a giraffe's.

"So you're taking flying lessons?" Just as I finish my sentence, the phone rings. The caller hangs up when the answering machine clicks on.

"I'm done. Just waiting for my FAA check ride. I'll probably get on with Air Transport or Quick Jet. I know a guy at Quick Jet who was hired a few months ago. He thinks he can get me on."

"That's great." I'd always hoped to travel and see the world. Mark knew that I'd applied to be a flight attendant. Odds were he was just sprinkling salt into an old wound that had already formed a tough scar. Like most sociopaths, he could sense weakness and extort its desperate bobbing and gulping from the shore while firmly grasping the life preserver.

I recalled when I believed every word that came out of his mouth; when I needed to think he was real; when he could rescue me from the worst days or darkest nights. I needed the sweet nothings—which was ironically what they were. I needed the lies and the support. He had played to my deficiencies and lack of self-worth. I'd wanted the closeness; the reassurance that I was loveable; the clean soapy smell of him next to me.

"So what are you up to?" he probes, sitting down on the other end of the couch Another call rings in the background. Once again, they hang up.

"Oh, not much. I still work for Guardian and I take graduate classes at night." I don't tell him that I'd only completed two classes and I could only handle one class at a time. The less he knows the better.

We'd met our senior year of high school and I became one of the many girls who'd seen their infatuation with Mark turn into

36

a torrid love affair. He was tall, cut, and wickedly charming. I was self-conscious and awkward—immediately drawn toward the confident way he moved and the dissolute way he lived. He knew the rules—they simply didn't apply to him. He drove fast. We'd only been together a few months, when I suspected that my perfume wasn't the only one he found irresistible, but a year later when he asked me to marry him, I was certain I'd been wrong.

"When I saw your mother, and she said you were coming into town, I got the idea she wanted me to call you."

"Yea, you know my mother. She always liked you."

"She looked good. Does she still teach yoga?"

"Yes. I think it's her fountain of youth." So, is he interested in my mom now?

"I saw your brother at Home Depot. Did he tell you?"

"I think he did. He lives at the hardware store since he bought a rent house." The phone rings again. The answering machine picks up.

"Marcus, I kept the baby awake. Where are you?" A woman's shaky, desperate voice echoes over the answering machine's speaker.

My mind wandered…"Where have you been?" I'd asked Mark on a late night winter's eve, years before. "I thought you were coming home after you got off work."

"There was terrible accident. A commercial glass truck ran into a semi and the driver behind him was decapitated. I had to stop—the cops weren't even there yet. It just took a while."

"Oh my God! That's awful. Where was this?"

"Over on the boulevard, near the paint store," he offered.

This exchange was only one of countless lies that characterized Mark and eventually poisoned our marriage. Mark had something for everyone. He could be respectful and mature around parents, warm and funny toward your younger siblings, and polished and professional at work. Mark was a man for all seasons—especially if the wind blew in someone new.

The voice on the machine is Stephanie Cochran's. Stephanie was my best friend in college and Mark's second wife. I'd learned to live in the darkness of Stephanie's shadow. She was blonde, tiny, and cute. She had a spray-on tan and white teeth. All the boys were in love with her. She'd flirted with Mark all during college. A month after Mark and I broke up, they'd gotten engaged.

"She is driving me crazy," Mark says, nodding toward the machine.

I hate Stephanie. I have so little and she had so much. She wanted my husband and I wanted to rip out her bleached hair. Mark had even called me several times after he told me they were getting married. Once he said he was going to dump her as soon as her dad got him on at FedEx…then he told me he'd made a huge mistake…that Stephanie was a spoiled brat…that he still loved me…that she would be out of the picture soon. Twice I'd called him back, only to have her answer the phone and start yelling and swearing. After that phone call, I left a note on his car. He called me, apologized for Stephanie's behavior, and said she was pregnant.

A month later, they were married. Bouts of nausea punctuated my own misery. I lost ten pounds. Then Mark called to tell me that Stephanie had a miscarriage. A year later, when Stephanie gave birth to a girl, I considered ending my torment permanently. The thought of Stephanie and her baby—his baby—and what should have been "my life" was devastating. Mark had told *me* he didn't want children. I wondered what he told her.

I prayed for the strength to end my own suffering, but it never came. Then Mark dumped Stephanie as soon as their baby was born. Maybe that was why I agreed to come over—to see what all my tears were about—or to see if I'd healed.

"How is your daughter?"

"She's fine. Stephanie's mother spoils her rotten."

"She's three months old, how spoiled could she be?"

"Oh, they hold her 24/7. They give her a bath every time she poops her diaper."

"Sounds like they are just trying to be good parents. Do you ever take care of her?"

"I won't be able to take her out for an unsupervised visit for awhile. Stephanie's determined to have complete control. Her mother is behind it all."

After our breakup, I became depressed, rarely slept and couldn't eat. He'd told me I was fat; said he didn't love me. He criticized my housekeeping, my cooking, and my taste in music. He thought I was boring. He wanted to try new things.

A noise interrupted my mental browsing. Someone was pounding on the front door. I got up to refill my water glass while Mark jumped off the sofa. I heard him open the door.

"Hi," he said, in a flat monotone.

"You said you were coming over after work," Stephanie said in an anxious flurry of words.

"I have company. Sarah dropped by. Come on in."

Stephanie walks toward me down the dark entry hall. When the lamplight hits her, I'm stunned. She doesn't look like the same person. Her too-thin frame has a deer-like quality. She's not wearing make-up and her sunken eyes have dark circle halos underneath. Mousy, thin, lifeless hair frames her face. She sits down on the sofa and issues a weak "hello." Stephanie looks like a heroin addict in baggy faded jeans and an old t-shirt with a hole.

I sink down nervously in a chair I'd custom ordered in another life. I still like the way the pattern plays against the sofa and the iron glass- top coffee table. I'd left all of my furniture, thinking that I might be moving back in. After all, furniture wasn't important, marriages were. I smile, not knowing the proper protocol for greeting the other woman.

"I waited for you. I kept the baby awake." Stephanie's face strains as she looks directly at him.

I wonder what lies Mark has told her? Did he tell her they would be back together soon? Did he make love to her and then leave her and go to another bed? Or was simply knowing he could twist and wring her heart like an old rag enough?

How does he live with himself? How does he sleep knowing how deep his lies cut into another's soul? I feel sorry for his baby daughter. I hope she doesn't grow up loving men who imitate the wretched heartbreak her mother has known.

I sit, sipping on the water, wishing I could castrate Mark the same way he mutilates the women in his life. I want him to know the same pain—the sleepless nights, and the self-loathing his victims experience. I want him to feel impotent and broken.

"Did your dad get the car started?" Mark says in Stephanie's direction.

"Stephanie's dad and I bought a Jaguar to restore," Mark relays for my benefit.

My own dad couldn't afford to restore a Jaguar. He's a blue-collar working stiff who's lucky to keep any savings at all. But Mark can talk paint off the wall. I wonder if Stephanie's dad still embraces their entangling alliance.

"He and my brother got it going today," Stephanie says in a weak breath.

I didn't want to stare at her. I knew she was a new mother who got no sleep. A new mother who had a child by a liar who made promises he didn't keep.

"So, how's the baby?" Mark says, finally acknowledging their relationship.

I can't stop the pity that tugs at my conscience.

"She was fussy today; I couldn't get her to settle down."

I could heal. I could change my phone number, move away, and start over. I could learn that I was too good to be in love with a worthless liar who made promises he didn't keep. I could raise my standards and become too good for the likes of someone like

Marcus Tyler, but Stephanie was trapped in an alliance for at least another 18 years.

"Who has her now?" he queries.

She can't hide. She is exposed like a gazelle on the Serengeti. The only protection she has is her parents and maybe a few lame laws that will force Mark to pay child support and then give him visitation. She will never be free. Every time she looks at her daughter, she will see small reminders of the man she will grow to hate. When she least expects it, his apparition will waft into her daughter's behavior, causing Stephanie to curse under her breath and strain to control words that want to spew forth.

"She has a name. Lindy was asleep when I left. My mom has her." She puts an uncomfortable emphasis on the word *Lindy* and speaks through clenched teeth.

Stephanie is caught in a vortex she might never escape. Somehow, I feel fortunate. I can rebuild my self-respect and leave my relationship with Mark to decompose like the rotting flesh of a corpse in the sun.

Shining an opportune light on what had really happened in the cold dark depths of my own personal hell *has* set me free.

"It's getting late. I need to go," I interject. "Good night."

"I'll walk you to the door," Mark volunteers.

"That's okay. I can see my way out."

On the Edge

I would have been better off locked in a dark basement by strangers in some remote Midwest countryside where the neighbors live too far apart to be nosy or maybe in a kibbutz growing organic asparagus. Anyplace on Earth would have been better than living with my parents.

Now days, observant teachers would call Child Protective Services; someone would have noticed the welts and the head jerks triggered by sudden movements close to my face. Mounds of cigarette butt-filled ashtrays, the lack of food in the refrigerator, and the worn out shoes would have tipped off mascara-wearing social workers—but there were no social workers or concerned teachers back then. People minded their own. No one worried about smoke-filled cars, children left unattended or hugs withheld. We were property. "Chattel," as our father often called us. He was the lord, while we enjoyed a rank closer to livestock.

The imperfections of my genome screamed their presence from the beginning. There was no ignoring the flaming red hair and the white skin of the ginger race: an ugly, sun-sensitive, child of a genetic aberration that should have never been. Granted, the evil lies in recessive underpinnings for generations. My parents hadn't known that on a hot drunken night in July they would conceive a colicky, dermatologically challenged son who would grow into an obese adult.

Even the owners of the all-you-can-eat buffet wince when they see me transport my three hundred-pound-plus King's Big and Tall-clad self into their restaurant. I feel like one of the giant inflatables flapping away at car dealerships on weekend sales with a generator filling the void between what is real and what isn't.

~~~

I'm standing at what must be one of the most beautiful views in the country. From the edge of the rocky outcropping I can see the huge valley below. To my right, the river culminates in groves of ash and wild blueberry before going underground. A field adorns the middle. Rows of golden-raked grain pull my eyes to the opposite side where summer growth blankets the steep slope with shades of deep green.

It's not a bad place to die. Peaceful.

Soon the early morning sun is warm and welcoming, calling me back to the primordial implosion that spawned life on this planet. I was never meant to live. Humans all think they are so damned important, unique, entitled. I know this isn't true. We are here as a guest of DNA seeking its own survival, not caring about the vessel, only about the lading. I couldn't deny there was a God; the sight before me is proof enough. I could deny our creator's concern for the individual. Who would have allowed the survival of my kind for so long?

The rock beneath my feet is starting to warm and the folds in my neck are sweating. The distance between it and the valley below is both dangerous and soothing. One more step and my problems are over. No more alimony or child support, no more pain, rejection or embarrassment. Freedom. I could forget about the warm flushes that betray my thoughts, the shyness that keeps me home, the people—staring…judging…criticizing.

The Earth would be my keeper. Insects would do their jobs, wild animals would be fed, and the soil would get its due. This is what nature intended. I am a crop, like the grasses in the field and the berries on a vine. It is harvest time.

I inch my way closer to the edge. The loitering trees below hold their boughs in an inviting embrace. A warm calmness drains from my head into the Earth below . . .

~~~

Leaving my refuge, the one place I could ultimately find peace, I head back to my car. I need to stop and get gas on the way to work. There are always open pumps at the station down the hill—one of the few good things about weekends.

The Gift

December 1968-Canyon, Texas. We are a nation at war. I'm in the third grade and it's the last day of school before the Christmas break. My class is celebrating the holiday with games and goodies. There is also a gift exchange with a three-dollar limit. My teacher, Mrs. Read, has assigned a number to each brightly wrapped present. Everyone in the class draws a corresponding number.

Mrs. Read asks us to go to the Christmas tree and find the gift with our drawn number on it. One of my classmates is upset. She has drawn her own gift. Mrs. Read asks us if anyone would like to trade with Karla. Everyone stares at her poorly wrapped, round present without a bow. No one offers to trade. The entire class stands clutching the cheap dime store toys like they are manna in the wilderness. Mrs. Read implores again through horn-rimmed glasses. No one budges. Mrs. Read's son is MIA in Vietnam, and her tolerance for selfish third-graders is low. Karla, the chubby kid with droopy socks, starts to cry. I spend the ticking seconds feeling Karla's pain. The look on her face is more than I can bear. The way Mrs. Read's eyes are glazing over tells me how disappointed and frustrated she is.

I offer my gift to Karla and take the paper-covered orb. Mrs. Read tells us to return to our seats and then we can open the packages. I tear off the tacky wrapping paper. Karla has given me a metal bank—shaped and painted like a globe. The local First National Bank gave them away to new account holders a few months before as verified by the logo on the base. My parents already have two of them at home. The other kids look at my bank and stick their tongues out like they had just licked the bottom of a shoe. I tell Karla thank you and try my best to smile.

I don't know if I am happy about doing the right thing or not. I take the bank home and my mother says she is proud of me. I'm still not sure.

December 1998-Yigo, Guam. I'm a guidance counselor at Yigo Elementary. I'm working with a class of third graders on a self-esteem project. We are making books about ourselves. Part of the project is to write something we have done that we are proud of. I love this project because in a community where 75% of the people live below the poverty level, it focuses on real human value—not on money. I show them what I wrote down as an example and tell them about Karla, her sagging socks and the metal bank. The entire class is mesmerized. Their teacher starts to cry. Now I'm certain that trading with Karla was the right thing. Some gifts take a long time to be appreciated.

Going Perfectly Straight

We are hiking enthusiasts. Okay, my husband is the enthusiast. I'm more like the underpaid Sherpa. He treks mountains and I watch for snakes on the local trails. But, occasionally, he and I go on small hikes together. So when he asked me to go on a quick hike late one afternoon, I was flattered. The sun was starting its western descent and the sky was pink with  anticipation. It was romantic, but not in the Cialis sort of way— more like Casablanca. Two people who just wanted to spend time together. It was an ideal evening for a leisurely stroll through the hillside.

We reached a beautiful valley we'd visited once before. The wildflowers were blooming and when the evening sun streamed across their petals, a fairytale sort of light filled the chasm. The only thing that didn't make it a white knight sort of experience was my husband's focus on his global positioning device. My husband's family loves gear, especially technical gear. So, the GPS was like discovering a way to eat without gaining weight. They couldn't get enough. There were the myriad of GPS-themed books. There was geocaching or treasure hunting using GPS coordinates, and websites that expounded the use of GPS for hiking and travel. The newest GPS accessory was software, given to my husband by his dad that mapped out hundreds of hiking trails in our local area. I wasn't worried; my husband was a professional pilot. He navigated for a living.

Very quickly, the romantic hike became a test of his latest technology. My husband didn't notice the wildflowers or their dazzling conspirator—the evening sun. He only saw the two-inch by two-inch screen he held in his hand. He led us over the next hill and toward a farm area I'd never seen before. There were white rail fences and small barns. We walked and walked and walked. We crossed several other trails, but my husband said that according to the GPS they weren't the right ones. We walked some more. We finally climbed over a fence that was posted with a "No Trespassing" sign. We continued down the other side of the valley past a sign that read "Trespassers will be shot on sight."

"Did your dad get that software package on sale? Because I'm pretty sure no one has used this trail since the landowner applied for a gun permit," I said. The trail became smaller and smaller and eventually became completely overgrown. Clearly, the bunnies and the coyotes were still using it, but it wasn't suitable for bi-ped species. My husband was becoming annoyed.

"That's the trail," he said, pointing and jabbing his finger toward the tunnel through the heavily overgrown brush. "Seventy-five feet that way and we pick up a trail that takes us home. You can see our house, right?"

I could see our house. Probably a little over a mile away, directly below the hill we were standing on, was a place where I could sit down, have a drink of ice water and tell my teenagers they were having cereal for dinner. "So, let's just head through this tunnel…think like a bunny," I said.

We crouched down and began the crawl that would get us closer to home. We were only about ten or fifteen feet into the tunnel when my husband yelled, "Abort! Abort! We gotta get outta here, somethins' crawling all over me!" Feeling I was trapped in a computer game and the enemy had just advanced, I backed out of the tunnel like I was leaving a fire.

Once I stood up. I could see that my husband was stripping off his clothes faster than a pole dancer at a sailor bar. In his defense, he was right. Ticks were crawling all over him. I immediately began to remove the quick little bugs from the naked man jumping around in front of me. I don't know why, but none of the bloodsuckers were crawling on me.

After Christopher Columbus had gotten dressed, we went back the way we came, but took a different trail toward the farming area we'd already traversed. We finally came upon a small barn with an animal standing in a fenced yard. "OMG, how lost are we?" I shouted.

"What is that anyway? A llama?"

"It's a freakin' alpaca! We are so lost that we have found an alpaca. How far have we hiked?"

"Aren't alpacas native to South America? According to the GPS, we've only traveled eight miles so far. We are nowhere even close to Peru yet."

"I know we aren't in a plane, Dexter, but thanks for the update."

"In fact, since there's a road here, we could probably call a cab."

"And tell them what? Do you see any street signs?"

"Well, maybe I could just give them GPS coordinates?"

At this point, I was thinking of orifices where I could place the GPS unit so it would be safe until the sheriff found my husband's cold, dead body. "Let's go back the way we came," I suggested, smiling broadly.

"It's getting dark," my husband pointed out.

"Don't you have at least one of those ten-thousand flashlights your father has given you over the years?"

"Well, actually there is one on my GPS."

I was pretty glad I hadn't secured the GPS unit in the safe place I'd thought of earlier. "So, let's go. Turn off the GPS. We might need the power for the light."

"I did bring extra batteries."

"Okay, MacGyver. Let's head back toward an area we are more familiar with."

About a half a mile back on the trail, we saw a coyote standing on the path. He stared straight at us with eyes that glistened in what light remained. He didn't seem frightened at all. In fact, he didn't even move. I think he was considering us for his dinner, either that or he'd heard gossip that the dumbest creatures on two feet were in his neck of the woods and he wanted to see it.

Finally, the coyote relented to let us scoot by and we kept walking until we ran across a more familiar trail. As soon as we approached a recognizable area, I asked my husband how far we had gone so far.

"About ten miles. How far do you think we are from home?"

By then, he'd relented to let me lead the way. "About three miles," I said. "You are going to have to whip out that light here before too long because it's going to be downhill."

"No problem. I have extra batteries," he said, again.

"Shut up before I stuff those batteries down your throat."

"Speaking of throats, are you hungry?"

"Am I hungry? I could make the Donner Party look like they were at a wine tasting."

"I have a Power Bar you can have."

"Well, thank you. But do you think you can fix this with an overly processed, overly priced candy bar?"

"No, you're right. How about a margarita?"

"How 'bout two margaritas, chips and salsa, some enchiladas, and all the sides at that place where the dog sleeps in the bar?"

"It's getting late," he said, turning on the anemic flashlight. "Will they still be open?"

"If we go straight there."

"But don't I need to take a shower? What if I still have ticks on me?"

"We'll eat in the bar. The dog won't mind."

The Trick

I entered the room and immediately began to remove my clothing and slid into bed next to him. I wanted to turn and face the wall and succumb to the nothingness of sleep, but I wouldn't. Even though I was exhausted after errands, cooking and laundry, I scooted closer and ran my hand across his hairy chest and down his rounded belly. I nuzzled against his cheek and began kissing his leathery neck. He took a deep breath at my familiarity and rolled toward me to embrace my form. I knew what to do.

He always responded like a well-timed pot roast, falling limp in places and maintaining integrity in others. I traveled to places I'd visited hundreds of times. All too well I knew the map of his body—the nape of his neck, the curve of his shoulder, the texture of his back that had seen far less sun. The finer hairs that occupied his forearms compared to the coarser ones on his chest were as predictable as the tide.

His breathing quickened as it always did when I slid my attentions lower. His belly shuddered as my hand moved over it. He touched my hand and slid it lower. I knew what to do. I always knew what to do.

Our bodies became a well-oiled clock. He was good for several minutes of tick-tock before the final strike. It was a predictable interlude. Nothing new. No videos or toys. I checked off the to-do list in my head while his body responded to every tick. He liked to have his ears licked. I never knew why, but it seemed a simple gesture. The wetness always got him closer. He wanted on top, which took less energy on my part except that right near the end he liked my legs wrapped tightly around him. He was a big man and almost crushed my body while his arms pulled my hair. He was always exhausted when it was over and kissed me twice and fell asleep in my arms.

I would slip out and leave the key card on the nightstand as I picked up my money—five new crisp one hundred dollar bills. I slipped out without notice. Until next time.

Double Stuf Oreos

I woke up when morning sunlight streamed in my lone bedroom window. I opened my eyes to an all too familiar sight. On top of the bedding covering my body were at least six banana peels. I hated these days. I would spend wasted hours trying to figure out what had happened during the night, and if I owed apologies to anyone. Furthermore, I usually avoided eating the very end of a banana. It was one of those food quirks from my childhood that I'd never gotten over and I could tell by looking at the peels that the entire white of the fruit was gone. The end of a banana usually has a coarser texture and sometimes it felt positively gross when I tried to chew it. So, I knew that I wasn't functioning in my normal capacity if I'd eaten the entire thing.

I picked up most of the banana remnants after I sat up. I hurried to the bathroom trash and discarded the smelly garbage, then went back to my bed and looked for stragglers. Once I was certain the peelings were mostly gone, I pulled the bedding off and loaded up the washing machine. *No more stringy banana bedding today.*

I started a pot of coffee, and then took out a cereal bowl and poured myself some Cheerios. The "Os" did not look particularly appetizing. As I poured the milk, I looked over at the bowl on the counter where I kept bananas. Yes, I'd eaten every single one. No wonder I wasn't hungry.

I'd been a sleepwalker or somnambulist as a kid. Friends and relatives would tell stories about finding me outside on the lawn with my pillow. Once my parents had even located me in the dog house after a frantic search. At my grandparents' house, I was known to get in bed with my grandmother. It wasn't until I started to live on my own that my nighttime adventures centered around food. The scariest incident was about two weeks before when I woke up with an empty bag of Double Stuf Oreos.

I'd never been a huge fan of Oreos. When I was a kid, my little brother would dunk them in milk and then drip the whole mess to his mouth. Our entire childhood he had worn chocolate-stained t-shirts. But, the worst part about the empty bag was that I'd never bought Oreos….

Okay, so how did I end up with an empty bag of Oreos? At first I thought I must've had company who'd brought them. But a text to all of my cohorts yielded no results. Maybe I'd borrowed the cookies from my neighbor while sleepwalking. Once, Franklin with the loud TV, had loaned me a garlic clove, so maybe they came from him.

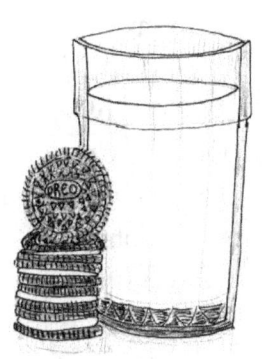

A few days after the Oreo incident, I went into the convenience store around the corner. Chuy, the clerk, asked me if I'd enjoyed the cookies. I normally only got gasoline from Chuy, but this time he was friendlier, more talkative. I didn't ask him if I had been in my pajamas when I'd purchased the Oreos, nor did I ask him how I'd paid. I just smiled, nodded and made my exit in record time.

The bananas were a different story. I always kept bananas in my apartment, and at last count, there were six. I'd eaten all six. And it was the third time I'd gotten up in the middle of the night to eat bananas.

I poured myself a cup of coffee and grabbed the container of 100% purely artificial hazelnut-flavored creamer. It was empty. I never put empty containers back in the refrigerator—that too was my little brother's MO. What had I done with the creamer? I knew it was at least half-full. Did I drink it? Pour it out? Fortunately, I always kept a spare. After a couple cups of coffee, I went and moved my sheets to the dryer. I hadn't been back in the kitchen but a few moments when I heard a thud from the utility room. I knew the sound. I used to use tennis balls to fluff my pillows—but I hadn't done that in a while. I hurried to the dryer and opened the door. I pulled on the wet bedding until something hit the floor. I looked down; what I saw didn't belong to me.

I put the sheets back in the dryer and leaned over and picked it up. The phone looked a little beat up—I'd definitely washed it with the sheets. I shook it, but no water came out. I hit a couple of buttons, but no lights came on and no sounds were emitted. I'd killed it. Whomever it belonged to, wherever it belonged, it was now dead. Boy, was I gonna have some explainin' to do. First I decided to text everyone I knew…and…do what? I couldn't confess that I'd found a strange cell phone in my sheets…

I finally noticed that the next day was the first day of spring. I would wish everyone I knew a "Happy Spring." The person who didn't get back to me might be the person to whom the phone belongs! It was genius. I set up a text on my own phone to be sent the next morning. By noon, I'd have my answer.

On the way to work the next day, I stopped in to get coffee. The convenience store keeps fresh fruit in a basket on its counter. Sometimes I also grab an apple for lunch. This time, Chuy smiled and asked me if I needed a banana. OMG. Did I have Chuy's cell phone? Chuy was nice, and he was really cute for an Asian kid who was about 19 years old and weighed all of 110 pounds soaking wet. What had I done? I could never go back in that convenience store again. Note to self—find a new place to get gas.

By lunch, no one had responded to my text message. I was starting to panic. Had I sent out offensive messages to all my friends while I was asleep? What could I have possibly said to insult everyone I knew? I had to find out whose phone I had.

I bought four boxes of baking soda. I'd seen a technique on a crime show that might restore the phone to health. I buried it in the white powder and hoped I could revive it by drying it out. There were still no responses to my text messages and soon I was running low on gas.

I realized that finding a convenient gas station in my neighborhood was easier said than done. With all the medians and one-way streets, I had to drive about ten minutes out of my way to fill up. What had I done to my safe "convenient" life? Surely, Chuy didn't work all the time. Maybe I could just get gas when he wasn't there.

All was quiet for the next few days, which wasn't unusual for the beginning of the week. People got busy at work; the Monday and Tuesday night television line-up was worth watching. By Wednesday I was ready to dig out the phone and interrogate it.

The baking soda had made a mess of its own. I used my blow dryer and a paintbrush to get the fine powder out as much as I could. Still nothing. Then it occurred to me, what if the battery was just dead? I took the battery out and brushed it off. I had a couple of old chargers in a junk drawer. I dug around, found one that fit, plugged it in and waited. It might be hours before it was charged— plenty of time to find other uses for the remaining baking soda.

After, I'd cleaned out my refrigerator, refreshed the garbage disposal, I was ready to see if there were any clues to the phone's ancestry. It perked right up when I pushed a button. First, I went to the messages menu—good, I wasn't locked out; no password required. There was only one voicemail and no text messages. I listened to the voicemail. It was man's voice, or maybe a deeper woman's voice, maybe a smoker or someone on hormone replacement therapy. Whoever it was, he or she should see a doctor. I couldn't understand anything on the message.

Who could I have possibly have brought home who had only one message? What about contacts? I went to the contact list—nothing. The person had to either be a loser or someone with OCD who kept their message box cleaned out.

What had I done? A lot of Asian people are very efficient. And what if your relatives were illegal? You wouldn't keep them in your contact list. And Asian people are usually very smart— they could memorize all of those phone numbers. Oh no. I'd probably picked up Chuy and had his phone! How could I possibly fix this and keep it from happening again?

The next morning, I called my doctor. The least I could do was talk to him and see if he could give me a medication to ward off my sleepwalking or recommend a specialist who could handcuff me to my bed frame every night. I told the front desk it was an emergency, after all, the Oreos alone were a health risk.

Doctor Seeth (pronounced seethe) was very thorough. I'd be lucky if I left there without a CAT scan or MRI. Certainly at least a full blood panel. "How are you?" he asked, walking in. Knowing full well that doctors hate patients who talk too much, I spilled my whole sordid story anyway, even the part about Chuy.

"Well, first, I'd like to thank you for the 'Happy Springtime' text," he said.

"You got it?" No one else did, or if they did, they didn't tell me. Dr. Seeth was cool.

"You've had sleepwalking episodes on and off since childhood?" He was making notes now.

"Yes, but never eating episodes. I never went to a store," I said.

"Okay, something is probably triggering this. Have you been under a lot of stress?"

"I've been trying to lose weight."

"What for?"

"It's a wedding. I'm in a coworker's wedding. I look like a bloated gorilla in the dress she picked out."

"That would explain the bananas," he said, smiling.

"What do I do?" I said with a pleading tone.

"Well, first you need to stop starving yourself. It could be messing up your digestion, causing reflux or changing up your sleep patterns. Both of those can cause sleepwalking and maybe the eating. I've never really had a sleep-eater. I'm going to give a prescription, and you can try that for a few weeks. There is an alarm pad you can sleep on designed to wake you up if you get out of bed until we get this under control."

"Are you serious? It's that easy?"

"Well, maybe. But, we'll keep you safe until we figure it out."

As I was walking to my car from the doc's office, I felt so much better. I could go to the convenience store and explain my problem to Chuy and give him his phone back and ask for forgiveness. I had a medical excuse, *a doctor's note.* I wasn't a hussy, as my grandmother would say. I'd head over there right now, even though I didn't have the phone with me.

Once I pulled in the parking lot. I started to lose my nerve. I could see Chuy's spiked blond hair behind the counter. Mmm …I had to do it before I chickened out and before I ran out of gas.

I parked my car and forced a smile on my face. I could do this. I had medical science in my corner. "Hi!" Chuy said, as I walked in the door. "Did you get that phone working?"

"What phone?" I said innocently.

"The one you bought from me the other night? You said your brother dropped your phone in his milk? The night you bought the cookies?"

"Oh, ya!" I said a little too loudly. "I did. Thank you very much. I had no idea you guys even sold phones."

"You'd be surprised at how many we sell. You can just pop your SIM card in and keep going."

"Wow…wow…thanks for all your help."

Shocked, I almost didn't make it to my car. Boy, did I have a lot of explainin' to do. It's a good thing my phone worked.

The Bee List

I walked into the house with two armloads of groceries. My son was sprawled on the couch and didn't offer to help. Jason was deep in the throes of adolescence and spent most of his time locked in his room ignoring us by keeping his earphones in. He glanced in my direction, barely acknowledging my presence. I'd gone from mommy to warden in less time than it takes to Google "adolescent depression." My return to work had created distance between us; I was never there when he got home.

My teenage daughter walked in and began searching through the bags.

"Get any cereal?" she said.

Marissa, almost sixteen, was certain her brother and sister had been a deliberate attempt to destroy any chance of only-child happiness she could've hoped for. I'd been an only child, certain that my parents had been selfish in denying me the sibling I longed for. That irony was lost on my own children.

"There are more bags in the car," I said, hoping for help. I turned to walk back to the driveway.

By the time I arrived, Marissa was digging through the grocery bags in the car.

"Why don't you just carry it in and then look for the cereal?"

"Mom, I'll starve by then."

"Well, you're not going to eat it here in the driveway. Take the bag inside."

"Why doesn't Jason have to help?"

"I'm going to recruit him next."

"Jason, get out here right now!" Marissa yelled, in her loudest cheerleader voice.

"Shhh. The neighbors don't need to know you are training for a hog-calling contest. Anyway, your brother has earphones in. He can't hear you."

I carried another bag into the kitchen past the stunt-double corpse of my son. I walked over to the couch. "Hey, why don't you help me carry the groceries in?"

Jason reached up and pulled out an earbud, after giving me an annoyed look. "Why can't Marissa do it?"

"She is, and you're going to help her. Come on. Don't you want to know what kind of cereal I got?"

"Mom, I don't really care," Jason said.

"I know, dear. That's why you're my favorite."

Two hours later, we were sitting at the dinner table when my youngest, Casey, walked in the door. "Where have you been? I told you we were having dinner together," I said.

"I just forgot. Hailey and I were studying for the spelling bee. It starts tomorrow."

"The bee is tomorrow. Why haven't you said anything? Do you want a whole piece of chicken?"

"It's just the classroom one. Whoever wins will be in the whole third grade one on Friday. Don't give me too many carrots," she said, wincing.

~~~

"Momma, momma, guess who won the spelling bee? I beat everyone in my class!" Casey's voice grew louder and louder as she ran down the hallway.

"Good for you! So now you have to be in the Friday spelling bee?"

"Mom, I don't 'have to.' I *get* to! I beat everyone in my class."

"Great! Are you going to study some more?"

"The teacher gave me a whole list of words. She said I have to know them all by Friday." Casey pulled out a stack of stapled paper and handed it to me.

I looked over the first page—two columns of numbered words. There were over a hundred spelling words. I kept turning the pages. There were six papers. I couldn't figure out how a third grader could even begin to learn 600 words by Friday.

"You're going to have to work on these every night," I said, remembering when Casey wanted to learn to play the piano. After the first lesson, she was ready to quit. After the second one, she did.

"Okay. Will you help me?"

"Sure," I said, hoping my desperation didn't show. How was I going to cook dinner, do laundry, run Jason and Marissa back and forth, and teach Casey the Bee List?

My husband had died in an industrial accident six months before. I'd found myself drowning in responsibilities simultaneously suffocating in grief. I hoped Casey couldn't detect the hesitation in my voice. She hadn't done anything wrong and I tried to protect her from the despair I'd felt since Allen's death. I'd learned to swallow my real emotions. As the family's primary buttress, I hid the crumbling foundation I'd built my facade on.

~~~

I had just dumped the last of the snow peas, into the pan where I was stir-frying, when Casey crawled up on a barstool.

"Momma, you said you'd help me with these words."

"Have you written any of them?" I asked, buying myself some time.

"I wrote all of these," she said, pointing to the first column.

"Okay, let's see here. How do you spell 'kudos?'"

"Kudos, k-u-d-o-s."

"Very good. Do you know what it means?"

"Mom, they don't ask us that."

"But you need to know what it means."

"Why?"

"Because, otherwise you'll never be able to use the words in stories."

"Mom, I just need to spell them. It's called a spelling bee. Not a story bee," she said, a whine in her voice.

"Casey, you need to know what the word means." I vigorously stirred the vegetables. A few of them slapped the side, splashing oil over the edge.

Jason walked in the door and dropped his backpack and hoodie on the floor.

"Jason, pick that stuff up right now and take it to your room," I ordered, my voice rising to a crescendo of irritation. My husband would've taken over the stir-fry or the spelling words. At the very least, he would have assumed the position of gatekeeper and directed Jason and his stuff out of the middle of the floor. I was just a tired, frustrated mother who didn't want to break her foot when she walked in the door.

"You don't have to be so mean," Jason said.

"Yes, I do. It's my job," I said removing the rice from the burner. By this time, the vegetables were begging for mercy and I turned the fire off.

"Momma, give me another one."

"What does kudos mean?"

"I don't know what it means," Casey shot back.

"It means 'good job' or 'good for you,'" I said firmly.

"No wonder, I don't know what it means. I never do anything right." Casey jumped off the chair and ran down the hall.

I took a deep breath.

"Could you please go help her with the spelling words?" I said in Jason's direction, knowing he would rather have his eyebrows shaved off than help out around the house. I began to scrape food into bowls and look for clean forks in the dishwasher.

He lowered his head and walked toward the hall. I didn't know if he was pretending not to hear me, or if in his adolescent stupor he actually hadn't.

The next night Casey didn't ask me about her spelling words. I carried laundry and put away dishes without the pages of the Bee List shoved in my face. Once I had finished the basic chores, I asked Casey if she wanted to sit down and go over the spelling words.

"No. Momma. I already did my words," she said.

"But don't you want to spell them aloud?"

"I already did. Jason helped me."

"Not today's list. The second page."

"We did it. When Jason got home, he helped me."

"Well, let's go over them again. I still want you to know what the words mean."

"Jason tells me. Then he asks me to use them in a sentence."

"Okay. If you think that you know them."

"Yup. I know 'em."

It was only third grade. She didn't have to be the world's best speller. Jason could barely spell his own name. If it weren't for spell-check he'd never have passed the sixth grade. But he did have the words right in front of him...

That night, exhausted, I went to bed early. I sensed Allen next to me and fell asleep, imagining his scent on the pillow.

I awoke to a noise down the hall. I slipped out of bed and moved toward the doorway. A faint light radiated from under the girls' closed door.

"Celebrity, c-e-l-e-b-r-i-t-y," I heard in hushed tones.

"Farthing, what's a farthing?" Marissa asked.

"It's British."

I was stunned. Maybe I was dreaming? What's a farthing? Surely, I'd heard incorrectly. Why would a third grader know what a farthing was. How would Marissa know what a farthing was? I went back to bed, hoping that Dickens might visit my dreams and clear it all up.

The next morning, I was still thinking about the *dream*. If Marissa and Jason were helping Casey, was I off the hook? Marissa had a new crush every week; how long would it be before Connor or Justin or Taylor replaced Casey's bee list?

Friday morning. I scrambled eggs for breakfast. The kids were quieter than normal. I heard Casey tell Jason "thank you." Odd. Then Marissa volunteered to walk Casey to school, even stranger.

∿∿∿

"Momma, Momma. I'm the best speller in the third grade!" Casey's voice rang out like an order of scattered, smothered, and covered at a Waffle House.

"That's great!" I said. "What's next?"

"I get to spell against all the other schools." Casey was beaming.

"Well, when does that happen?" I said.

"I have a paper and more words. It tells all about it."

The district bee was only a week away and there were over three hundred new words on the list. I hated to see Casey get her hopes up. The chance of her winning was so remote. She had never been a straight-A student and spelling had never been one of her best subjects. Yet, there was a spark in her I hadn't seen since Allen's death.

∿∿∿

I continued to give Casey words from the Bee List when I could, but Marissa and Jason had taken the brunt of the tutoring. The worst part about the bee list was that Casey still had all of her

66

regular homework. She had always struggled in math, unlike Marissa and Jason.

"Dugong," I said.

"Dugong, d-u-g-o-n-g," Casey answered.

"Quisling."

"Quisling, q-u-i-s-l-i-n-g. Do you know what quisling is, Mom?"

"Yes, a quisling is a part of a feather."

"No, it's not. Even Jason knows what a quisling is."

Just then, Jason walked in the door without dropping his book bag in the immediate vicinity.

"Jason, Mom doesn't know what a quisling is," Casey said.

Jason looked in my direction. "You're kidding right?"

"And I suppose you know what a quisling is?" I said, shaking my spatula at him.

"Sure. It's someone who collaborates with a political enemy. Named after some Norwegian fascist during World War II." He continued walking toward his room without slowing his stride.

I dropped the spatula. I could feel the pain of stupidity splatter on my leg. Did my son just say something he couldn't have seen on Facebook?

"Casey, sweetheart, do you have any math homework tonight?"

"Yes."

"Why don't you see if your brother will help you while I clean up this mess?"

"Okay, Mom."

~~~

The day before the district bee, we had gotten up early. Jason and Marissa were taking turns with the Bee List and I was off to work. By then, every spare moment in our house was consumed with the spellings of umlauts, graupels, and trepaks. We had become a spelling machine. Casey was becoming more and more excited. The rest of us had amped our vocabularies and developed an intimate knowledge of words we could never use in mixed company. We had created our own special language, like identical twins. We had come together in ways that only lovers of Pig Latin could understand.

By lunch, I was making plans for the state finals. I would have to take off work and buy something new to wear. What do the mothers of spelling bee champions wear? Something dark and professional or something soft and demur? Demure, d-e-m-u-r-e. The whole experience had become subjugating, s-u-b-j-u-g-a-t-i-n-g…no, really, r-e-a-l-l-y….

At 3:30 p.m., Marissa called. "Mom, Casey is sick. Her face is red and she says she is having trouble breathing."

"Take her temperature. Go get the thermometer from the box under my sink, and call me back."

Should I leave work right now? Casey never gets ill. Call me back. Call me now. Now, damnit.

"Mom, she has a temperature of 104 degrees!"

"Is she still have trouble breathing?"

"She keeps taking little breaths—I don't know!" Marissa's voice was urgent.

"Call 911! I'll leave right now. It'll take at least twenty minutes for me to get there. Ask them where they are taking her." I hung up, grabbed my purse and didn't take another breath until I merged onto the freeway. I panicked…Allen, I can't do this by myself. Why did you have to leave me? I wasn't cut out to be a single mom. Casey has to be okay. . .

Someone must have known that a crazy woman had been unleashed on the road. Traffic was light and I made it home quickly. My hands were shaking as I turned down our street. The ambulance was parked in the driveway. The thought that Casey couldn't be transported flitted through my brain as I pulled in front of the house. Breathe. You have to breathe.

68

A paramedic walked out the door just as I was running up the walk.

"Is she okay? Where is she? Is she here?" I allowed no time for answers.

"Oh, I think she'll be fine. Her fever should start coming down and we are giving her some oxygen right now. We think—"

I shoved past him before he finished his sentence. Casey was lying on the sofa with plastic tubing trailing in all directions. She waved as soon as she saw me. I ran over to the sofa and brushed her bangs to one side with my hand. Casey had spots. Red blotches on her face and arms.

"We think she has chicken pox, the younger female paramedic said. "They're going around. She says she has never had them."

"No, she hasn't. But she's had the vaccine."

"It doesn't always work. We can take her in, if you want, but her fever has broken and she's been talking to us. She can spell contagious. That's a pretty good sign."

"No, I'm sure she'll be fine. Thank you for your help."

~~~

Just as the ambulance was pulling out, Casey wailed, "Mom, what about the spelling bee?"

"Next year," Marissa said. "You'll definitely win next year."

"Oh yeah, that gives us a whole year," Jason said.

"We are so goin' to nail it," I added.

Eureka

"Clara Jean, why don't you visit your sister this afternoon?" Mama's voice rings from the parlor.

"Because she's busy, Mama."

"Your sister always has time for you."

"Not since she had her baby. The little one takes all of her time and attention and all she ever talks about is her baby weight and how Russell don't help her none."

"Russell's a good man. Your sister is lucky to have him."

For a moment, I think I've won. That I'd exhausted Mama's stubborn quest to get me "out of the house" hoping I'd find my own Russell. Then Mama's voice chimes again, "San Francisco's got a herd of eligible bachelors, but you gotta get out to meet 'em. None of 'em knockin on our door unless you fancy up and leave this house!"

"Fancy up! Have you seen those bloodsuckers? Losers, the lot of 'em. Lookin' to git rich the lazy man's way. Niners. Wish I'd never laid eyes on this place." Papa, a would-be forty-niner, died within a month of our arrival. He was panning for gold on a hot July day.

"We's here now. Make the best of it."

I've lost this round, but fortunately, I have plenty of work, so I'm too busy for Mama's socializin'. My sewin' business is boomin', my reticule is fat with coins and gold dust. I'll buy my way out of this devil's paradise after next winter. No family tie is gonna keep me harnessed to this hell hole. Preachers and prostitutes be damned. I'm goin' back to my sweet Virginia where people still know what polite society is.

"Clara, could you go get us some venison for stew? Them turnips and onions need somethin'."

"Yes, Mama." Mr. Carlisle's market is just around the corner. I make about ten trips a week there since Mama never plans very far in advance.

"We live in the city now. We don't need that canning nonsense with a store next door," she says. I pin on my dark hat and grab my shawl; I slip out, planning to be back by the time the stove needs shovelin'.

At the market, I wait for Mama's meat. The old grocer is gone for several minutes. Wasn't thinkin' I'd see anyone in the small store, never did. Then Elizabeth Tallwaite breezes in.

"Clara Jean. Haven't seen you in a month of Sundays! Has your mama been sick? She wasn't at church last week."

"My, Lizzy, don't you look nice." I've learned to distract the church people, so I don't have to explain why I ain't been sittin' on them hard pews. In truth, I can't stand to sit there and listen to some preacher tell me how it's my job to get married and have young 'uns. My hips belong to me. I'll decide if they are for breedin' or not.

"Oh, thank you! My new gentleman friend is comin' to call this day. I want to look nice."

"Well, I'm sure he'll appreciate the effort." *I'll be out of here in a minute.* Just as I finish my thought, Mr. Carlisle returns. I place the nickel on the counter and turn to leave.

"Clara Jean." Lizzy's voice trills like a lark.

"Yes?"

"Would you care to join some of us for a sail around the bay this Friday?" My gentleman friend knows a captain and made special arrangements.

I'd rather have my head shaved. "Oh, what a dear you are! When are you setting afloat?"

"Around ten in the morning."

"Let me consult with Mother. I usually accompany her on Fridays."

"Excellent. I hope you can make it. Eli Halbeck will be there…he'd love to see you. He's so handsome these days."

Lizzy is always trying to match someone up. "Good to see you, Lizzy." I hold my head higher than usual walking out the door. *Elizabeth Tallwaite has nothing on me.*

By the time I reach home, Mama is scraping turnips and carrots for the stew. "What's the meat look like? The last batch was a little bitter."

"I haven't seen it. 'Twas already wrapped, didn't want to bother Mr. Carlisle more than I had to."

"He's gettin' old. Last time I don't even think he recognized me," Mama said, shaking her graying head.

"Saw Lizzy. She asked me why you twernt at church Sunday."

"Lizzy is such a sweet girl. You know there's a gentleman caller in her life."

"She mentioned as much. Tried to match me up with that Eli Halbeck on Friday."

"Is there a party? Clara Jean you have to go to parties."

"Not a party. Just a sail around the bay."

"A sail around the bay…you've never sailed. You must go. What a generous invite."

"I knew I shouldn't have told you. I don't need Lizzy's suitor service. I need to go back to Virginia and find myself a real gentleman."

"Clara Jean, you never know what Cupid has in store for ya."

"Cupid! Honestly Mama. You think Lizzy is Cupid? She *is* getting a little girth on her…probably should snag a man before she weighs more than a milk cow."

"That is no way to treat someone who invited you on an outing."

"Maybe this stew could use some of the dried rosemary?" I move toward the spice shelf. "I love the scent of it cooking."

"Perhaps it could."

My distraction habit works on Mama as well.

We finish eating the stew and sit in front of the stove for warmth. I have a basket of mending and Mama sits with the Bible open on her lap. The night air is chilly, but the fire warm. I weave small stitches across the mending gourd and dream about my sweet Virginia.

"Wear the chestnut dress." Mama's words seem spoken more to the fire than to me.

"For what?" I feign ignorance.

"The outing. The sailboat trip."

"I think the chestnut dress is tight."

"Wear it with your nice straw hat. It frames your face and will keep the sun off ya."

"Why should I have to sail with those pew polishers? If God intended fer us to be on the water, he'd have given us webbed feet."

"He did give us the sense to stay dry. You're goin' if no other reason than to be polite."

It's over. I'd lost. Why hadn't I kept my big mouth shut?

A frosty coolness settles in our small house. I refuse to acknowledge Mama's demands and she refuses to acknowledge my resistance. I awake Friday morning to the reddish brown dress pressed and hanging from the kitchen doorway.

I figure I can get dressed, leave the house and return in a few hours and Mama would never be the wiser. Except that damn Elizabeth Tallwaite would surely mention my absence to Mama on Sunday. Reluctantly, I dress and plop the dark straw hat on my head and tie its sash. I might have to go on Lizzy's excursion, but I don't have to like it. No one can make me like it!

I hail a coach to take me to the wharf and trudge along the boardwalk trying to ignore the fish smell while looking for Lizzy's auburn hair. She spots me before I see her and her new beau.

"Clara Jean, Clara Jean!" Again, the chirp of Lizzy's voice annoys my senses.

Waving my arm, I head in her direction.

"Clara Jean Trumbull, this is my friend Leo Philips."

"My pleasure, Miss Trumbull."

"And mine, Mr. Philips." *Who are you kidding?* Lizzy's gentleman caller is old enough to be her father. Niners! They find a few nuggets and think new boots and a waistcoat will buy 'em a wife.

"Come on Clara, we're over here. See the captain with the blue shirt?"

I stomp across the nasty ground and follow Lizzy to a smaller pier. I see Eli Halbeck standing near the man with a blue shirt. The pocks on Eli's face have cleared, but he still looks like a boy dressed in his father's clothes. He stands and walks to the front of the craft and helps me aboard. The step is steeper than I would have liked, but Eli has a firm grip so I step down without falling. Lizzy and I sit on the bench next to each other and look out at the busy port.

Four more young people from the church have joined us and I'm forced to relive the shaky boarding of the boat again and again. Finally, we are seated and the captain, who looks to be about a decade older than most of us, orders his first mate to untie the craft and shove off. The mate and the captain hoist the smaller sails and maneuver us out of the congested harbor. Larger sails are raised, and the boat picks up speed. Suddenly, the fishy stench of the boardwalk is gone. A crisp, fresh breeze blows my hat off, and it flops around, bound by the ties under my chin. The boat seems to lift and skims across the water. I am no longer a seamstress on the east side, but the guest of the sea. We all gasp as the boat slows to bounce over a rough wave. Sea lions bark along the beaches and the reedy grasses that jam the coves. We bring the boom around, catch another breeze and fly some more. I'd never really thought about how wonderful it would be to soar over the ocean like a bird looking down at fish and seaweed. I feel free for the first time since I arrived at this God-forsaken place.

"What do you think?" Lizzy says, holding her bonnet in place.

"That this is better than a train! No smell, no stuffy compartments."

"Yes, I suppose it is wonderful. My hair is getting into an awful mess, though."

"I feel like a bird. Like I can fly." The boat slows and we lap peacefully next to a pod of dolphins. I so envy them. No churches or bonnets. Just soothing water skimming over their smooth bodies.

Suddenly, a huge rush of water bursts from the surface. I feel panicky, then the captain shouts, "It's a humpback! A beauty!"

"A what?!" I shout to Eli.

"A whale, a humpback."

The enormous animal throws itself back into the water. It is bigger than a railroad car and powerful. I'd never imagined anything so breathtaking. And what keeps it from turning the boat over?

The captain says that humpbacks are one of over a dozen species of whales that roam the Pacific. I was familiar with whale oil, but I'd never envisioned the amount of effort it must take to obtain the fuel. The animal is massive; I feel so small and powerless next to it. I sit looking toward the horizon, hopin' for another glimpse of the huge creature. When I can't sit anymore, I climb up and stand on the narrow bench.

"Will it come back?" I ask the captain.

"I reckon we'll see it again. The whales seem as curious about us as we are about them."

I stand waiting. Just as I am about to sit, the boat steadily lifts with a large wave then suddenly plummets, leaving me several inches off of the bench in midair. I reach for the ropes tethered on the gunwale, but before I can grab one, water comes at me fast and hard with the force of a blizzard.

I'm gasping. I need to right myself and spit out the seawater in my mouth. I don't know if I'm the only one or if all of us have been pitched to our death. The skirt on my gown is like an anchor. I can swim, but not in a dress. I reach down and rip the stitches I'd so carefully needled less than a year ago. I hold my breath and tear enough away so I can tread water more easily. I see the boat not twenty feet away and move toward it. Eli throws off his father's coat and dives in the water, swimming toward me.

Once we meet, he shouts for the captain to move the rope ladder and we swim together, finally reaching the vessel. I grab the rope ladder and cling to it. Eli yells at me to climb while he wrings the water out of what is left of my skirt. As I clamber in, Lizzy is holding her shawl out and wraps me in it. "Oh my! Oh my! Are you sound? Will you ever forgive me?" There are tears in her eyes. Here I am, a drowned rat with everyone looking at my knickers. No hat, half a dress and feeling such a fool.

"I'm fine. Wet, but fine."

"We must get you home and into some dry clothes," Lizzy says.

The ride back to the wharf dries me out some and I feel the captain glance over my way and I see a smile out of the corner of my eye. Some nerve! It was his fault we drifted so close to the whale. By the time we reach shore, I'm only half-drowned. Lizzy and her beau escort me home and I try not to think about how

76

embarrassed I feel. It doesn't matter anyway. I'll be leaving San Francisco as soon as my purse is full. No whales where I'm going …or arrogant captains.

Mama is shocked at the sight of me. I duck upstairs while Lizzy explains the whole shameful situation. I hear Mama laugh as she closes the door.

"Clara Jean, dear, how about some warm soup?" Mama's voice travels up the stairs.

"Yes, that sounds good." I wish I were sippin' it on a ship bound for the East though.

By the time I finish the broth, I'm more than a little tired. The warmth of my bed is a welcome relief, compared to the cold ocean water I'd experienced a few hours before. I drift off to sleep, trying to bury the image of my soakin' self deep in the recesses of my mind—forgetting the whale, the captain and the perfect Elizabeth Tallwaite.

~~~

"Deeear, Miss Lizzy is here!" Mama's voice echoes off the bedroom door.

Why can't those two let me be! Didn't Lizzy get enough of the sight of me yesterday?

"I'll be right down, Mama."

I take my time hoping that Lizzy might give up and leave, but luck is not to be had.

"How are you? I feel so bad. I just had to come and see with my own two eyes that you are well." Lizzy sips tea from Mama's best teacup and seems truly contrite.

"I'm fine, Lizzy. I'll just remember to stay in my seat next time." *Like I would do it again!*

The girl doesn't stay long and I am quite relieved when she takes her leave. Later that day, I answer a knock on the door and find Eli standing there, hat in hand.

"Clara, I had to stop by and tell you how truly sorry I am. I should have stopped you."

"Eli, thank you for coming by, but I'm fine—really."

"You'll let me know if I can do anything for you or your mama?"

"How nice of you. But we are all right, surely." I begin to close the door, fearing that he expects an invite to tea. Fortunately, he takes the hint and leaves me to my privacy.

Mama sends me back to the store early in the evening and this time I am more careful. I wait down the street a piece to make sure no Lizzy Tallwaite or anyone else who'd heard about my spill is around. When I return home, I'm surprised to hear voices in the parlor. "Clara Jean, Captain Strauss has come to check on your condition."

Captain Strauss! My condition! Why I never…. The captain stands as I step around the corner. "Clara Jean, the captain here was just telling me why he came to California."

"Afternoon, Miss Clara. I'm glad you're feeling well."

Well! I wasn't sick. Haven't you people ever seen someone wet before! "Thank you Captain," I say, smiling.

"Now, tell us. Why did you come to California?" Mama says.

The captain looks down at the floor for a moment and then speaks. "I guess the same as everybody else. I wanted riches."

"And did you get your riches?" I say. I don't think the captain is rich, or even close to it.

"Well, I guess you could say I did. I may have come here lookin' fer gold but what I found was worth much more."

"What did you find Captain Strauss?" Mama leans in. I can tell she is curious about our visitor.

"I found this brand new state and the biggest trees in the world. Sequoias. Giants of the forest. Huge reminders that God is greater than us all."

"You didn't stay here cause of some big trees?" I say.

"No, but the tallest mountains in the country are worth staying for. The Sierras rise to almost 15,000 feet. The lowest point in North America, Death Valley, is nothing to ignore either."

A glint comes to his eyes. He is more handsome than I remember.

"The best farmland, the brightest sunshine, beaches and sea ports unlike any I'd ever seen. Glaciers, deserts and forests. The gold in California isn't the dust panned in the streams, it's the abundance of Mother Nature in all of her splendor—the whales, the dolphins, the bears. A place that hasn't been spoiled. Unlimited possibilities. To a man who isn't afraid of work, California is a king's ransom."

The captain seems younger and suddenly taller now as he sits up in the chair. He isn't the same man who smirked on the boat. "What about the boat? How did you come to own a boat?" I ask.

"Hundreds of 'em just abandoned. Importers got the gold fever and left 'em to ruin. My eureka moment had nothing to do with prospectin' but was the rescue of the *Kathleen*. We take passengers down to San Diego and Pueblo de Los Angeles, then carry another fare back. It's safer than horseback and stagecoach. Sometimes I drop anchor at one of the islands…had a fare to the Mission San Buenaventura once. The rail will be going down there soon enough, but for now I can get people down there and back faster than anything else."

"Do you often spot whales?"

"More often than not. Always see dolphins and sea lions."

The beauty of the ocean comes alive in the man's blue eyes. He doesn't stay much longer but invites me and Mama to come down to the wharf again, even recounts stories about he himself fallin' overboard. I don't feel as embarrassed as I did before.

I go to church with Mama on Sunday. Lizzy can't wait to sashay up to me on Leo's arm. "Clara Jean, you are looking well. I hope you'll forgive me for your accident."

"I'm as well as ever. I may even go for another sailing adventure. Your Captain Strauss invited me again to sail on his boat."

"Which boat? He has several, you know," Leo says, earnestly interested. "Now that he has the dry good business, he doesn't sail as much."

"Oh, I didn't know that." Captain Strauss was a man full of surprises.

I return to the wharf later that day. I hear the captain before I see him. With his sleeves rolled up, I notice that he is fit, not afraid of hard work. He is confident and strong, not desperate and dirty like the niners. I wave in his direction and he speaks to his first mate and steps off the boat to meet me.

"Miss Clara Jean, are you here for another swimming lesson?" His smile breaks into a set of straight white teeth.

"Captain, I figure you might need some lookin' after, seein' as you too have been known to fall overboard." His laughter rings off the bow; at once I feel comfortable. We sail out in a smaller boat called a yawl and I observe a pelican diving for food. Something about the captain makes me feel like anything is possible. Like dreams do come true. His spirit is infectious. I find out that his given name is Jonas and his mother was a dressmaker in Bavaria. He is kind enough to escort me home.

Mama invites him to dinner. He and I walk down to Mr. Carlisle's store. I feel comfortable beside him. He takes his coat off and puts it on my shoulders. We walk in rhythm, slowly, my arm linked in his. I almost pray to run in to Elizabeth Tallwaite.

This evening I can't help but wonder if the captain's California is the same one I know. *There is an energy here*, one that I have found annoying up until the present, but there are also opportunities and at least one gentleman. Captain Strauss and his brother are particularly successful. He asks me to come and work at his shop or at least sew for them in my home. He claims that his brother's waist-overall production needs the oversight of a woman, that there is more work than his brother can handle. He says that the garments are quite sturdy, practical to a fault almost. Perhaps I will take him up on his offer, call on his brother Levi, maybe California is the land of opportunity.

The Ticket

He had been working on the old lawnmower for well over an hour. It had been his experience that these infernal devices would last indefinitely if the oil was changed regularly and the blades were stored clean (barring the occasional rock hit that invariably bent the crank shaft). However, it had also been his observation that no one ever did this. Inevitably, do-it-yourselfers just wanted to get the job over with, and most landscape companies hire laborers ignorant of such things. Frustrated, he decided to break for lunch and start fresh in the afternoon.

Carlos had taken the maintenance job with the Wynns about six months after his wife had passed away. The emptiness of the home had grown to be too much for him. He found himself picking up the newspaper because Sophia had hated clutter. He would stand at the sink, her sink really, washing his supper dishes because she hated to wake up to dirty dishes. He continued to sleep on his side of the double bed. She wanted the side closest to the hall. In earlier times, there were babies in the adjacent rooms; babies who had needed soothing, holding, and feeding. Later on, there were nightmares that required calming, fevers that had to be checked, and doors that had to be latched behind absent-minded teenagers. It had been her side of the bed, her domain.

The ad had read: "Large estate needs groundskeeper. Position includes residence, vehicle, and benefits." It seemed to be the fresh start he needed. He called the number and Mr. Wynn had seemed pleasant and amenable. The vehicle turned out to be an old '88 Ford long bed, and the residence was actually the original farmhouse to the property. The benefits included an old bloodhound named Festus. The home was simple, like the dog. Carlos felt like it suited him. It reminded him of the home he grew up in. It was located on the back of the property and between it and the main house was about an acre and a half of grounds. There was a pool, a rose garden, and a small potting shed/greenhouse.

Carlos had never worked as a groundskeeper. He'd worked as a supervisor for the city's maintenance department, overseeing work crews for over twenty-five years and retired with a pension. He figured that somewhere along the way he had seen just about everything done wrong. He'd become a keen observer of people and politics and had experienced the human condition from its most basic level.

Carlos concluded that politics were basically vanity, balance, and money. Politicians had to first convince themselves that seeking public office was a purely altruistic endeavor, followed by the artful harmony of nobility and self-preservation, and finally, the realization that it all came down to money: budgets, campaign funds, taxes, and salaries. He'd decided early on that installing a quality culvert or knowing enough to plant wildflowers on fallow lots was far more substantive than speaking at the rotary.

Ultimately, he was in control of the outcome. He had the final responsibility. He enjoyed challenge and solid satisfaction. It was real to him: the smell of new soil, the cement he scraped off of his boots, the taste of sweat in the summer and that of coffee, while he waited for the snow plow to warm up in the winter. Yes, this job suited him. It was real.

Mr. George Wynn had once served on the City Council, and Carlos had vaguely recalled him from the introductory tour. He had seemed straightforward and logical and Carlos had figured that he probably wouldn't be good for more than one term, maybe two. Carlos respected him and upon his hiring, quickly dubbed him Mr. G., but spoke it in a soft, fatherly way.

He and Mr. G had personally removed the old oak tree that fell after a lightning strike. The large limbs had to be carefully separated with the chainsaw; each amputation caused the huge carcass to moan and writhe like a dying animal. They agreed to have the stump removed by a professional and replant the new tree themselves. Like any good public servant, they both knew when to contract a job out.

~~~

Carlos put the beans on the old stove, lit it, and opened the bag where he stored the homemade tortillas. One thing he refused to buy at the store was tortillas. He had learned to enjoy the dough in his hands and the smooth, elastic quality it acquired when he rolled out the balls. He had also found the mass-manufactured ones packed down to a composition more like cardboard than bread. He enjoyed the spongy thickness and texture as he gently tore them apart. It felt primitive and holy; the way bread was intended to be enjoyed.

~~~

The lawnmower finally came to life and Carlos was relieved. It had only taken two trips into town, but he thought proper care of the machine from here on out would prevent breakdowns, and he wouldn't feel so guilty about the wasted time. He knew so many people from his tenure with the city that trips to town were rife with social obligation: be it a nod or a full-scale bull session, it was never expedient. He had to get the lawn mowed before tomorrow's rain prediction.

It was the competition between him and Mother Nature he'd come to enjoy, each coaching the reluctant players to victory. She, with the power of the universe: the sun, the wind, the rain, and the insects and animals; he, with the manure, the irrigation, and the mulch. It was a game, and like any worthwhile endeavor, he both loved and hated it. One hundred percent victory would bore, one hundred percent defeat would devastate. The sparring continued.

Carlos had the luxury of using the truck for his own errands, something the city had forbidden. Mr. G had given him a card to charge the gas on. It was efficient and he liked the fact that he had earned his boss's trust.

The Wynn family had been good to him. He was invited to dinner regularly at the big house, and when Mrs. G. cooked a batch of something, she would send down a dish if he had declined her invitation. On this day, he had filled the old truck and was waiting inside the QuikMart line to pay. The line was unusually long and slow because the state lottery had grown to epic proportions and no one had won recently. The majority of the lottery profits were earmarked for education. Carlos found it ironic that those who funded math education must not have any, since the odds of winning were astronomical. It was a fools' game, and he was in line behind them.

Finally, it was his turn. "Pump 6," he informed the clerk. She gave him the total. He handed the card over and was quickly out of there. He carefully replaced the card in his wallet and on the way home he glanced at the receipt he had laid on the seat of the truck. There on the top of the gas ticket was a computer-picked lottery ticket.

"Damn," he thought. He hated the idea that they had charged Mr. G. for a $1 Super Lotto ticket and he felt embarrassed that Mr. G. would think he bought it on purpose. He would go by the big house on Monday and make it right. It really was no big deal. He put the grocery bag on the table and propped the ticket up between the salt and pepper so he wouldn't forget.

The next day he had decided to take it easy and work on the small hand-carved gifts he made for each of his grandchildren every Christmas. They were small gifts, some had engines, and some had paint. Some had been designed as miniature reproductions of opulent furniture for a grand dollhouse. Each was unique and designed for each of his four grandchildren based on their age and interest. He wanted them to remember their Poppy with these special treasures.

He had a small game, carved by his grandfather, in which large wooden balls had been carved inside an open box with depressions that could trap all the balls at once by a skilled player. Carlos had gotten the game when he was only four, but had not mastered it until he was ten. When his Poppy died, it had been the only thing that brought him comfort, and now in his sixties, he felt the same way as he glanced at its station up on the shelf, next to the refrigerator. He recalled how its waxy finish felt the first time his grandfather nested his big old hands around Carlos' small chubby ones to show him how the game worked, and how sometimes moving something a long way required a minimal tilt in the right direction, a lesson that had come in handy raising his children. A well-placed nudge seemed to motivate them far more often than a sweeping command or an ultimatum.

Carlos decided to watch the news before he went to bed. His hands were tired and he had to work tomorrow. As the old television warmed up, he could see the Super Lotto numbers already coming into focus on the screen. He grabbed the ticket resting between the condiments. He only caught the last four numbers. They matched. He wondered if he was just getting old or if the state lottery commission could only afford twenty seconds of air time. *Damn.* He would check the morning paper. It really wasn't much of a paper, but it did have the state lottery picks, the weather, the baseball scores, and a few other things you have no control over.

Carlos didn't know what time it was when he awoke. It was still dark and he felt wide awake. He shifted positions on the bed, purposefully moving his head to one corner and his feet to the opposite corner. He thought about the lottery ticket and tried to dismiss such falderal from his conscience. He had never won anything in his life. He only had four of the nine required numbers, and what would he do even if he had won? He could live anyway he wanted. He could help his children own homes and buy cars. Instead of carving small tokens for his grandchildren, he could buy them anything they wanted. Hell, he could buy anything *he* wanted. He could make all of their dreams come true: Ivy League universities, five-star restaurants, plasma televisions, hot tubs; his mind raced, there was no end to the things he could buy. He would move, there would be no need for him to work. He could afford a cook and housekeeper. He could drive a new truck. "Relax," he said to himself, "go to sleep." After all, he only had four of the numbers. He liked the moderate farmhouse. The wooden screen door made a friendly sound when it slammed. The creaky floor board in the hall had become familiar. He knew exactly how long it took the hot water to get to the bathroom. Festus patiently waited for him every morning and eagerly expected to accompany him on errands. His son lived in a small two-bedroom apartment, not far from the farmhouse, with his wife and three little girls trying to save enough money for the purchase of an old house they hoped to restore. His firstborn granddaughter had graduated as valedictorian of her high school class and was starting college on a full scholarship in the fall.

He was a simple man. He enjoyed the simple life he had here. He had someone who cooked for him. He enjoyed the gardens. He looked forward to the weekends when his grandchildren came and swam in the pool.

Carlos realized that for the first time since Sophia's death, he was content.

He was glad he had the time to carve toys for his grandchildren. He was proud of his son's determination. He knew his beautiful, smart grand-daughter would work hard in school. He knew he could keep the lawnmower going. He would teach his grandchildren how to make the light tortillas and watch their faces as they roll out the elastic balls. His mind was still spinning. He had to sleep, and he had to work tomorrow. Carlos felt his brain fighting the exhaustion that encompassed him. He had to rest. *Make it stop.*

Carlos awoke without feeling rested. He had to get the paper. He had to put on coffee. He had to let Festus in: it was raining. He opened the door and the old dog wandered in, leaving a trail of water on the wooden floor and filling the room with musty rankness. Carlos stepped out to the yard to retrieve the paper. The plastic-enclosed journal was partially soaked.

He went back into the house and began to separate the soggy pages. He was able to identify the lotto picks until he got to the last number. He checked the lottery ticket. All the digits he could make out on the soggy paper matched. He took a deep breath. His chest tightened. He would have to hurry. Drinking his morning coffee was a chore. His throat was tight; he could see the future hurling at him like a roller coaster. Once you climb on, there is no stopping. You hold on for dear life. You close your eyes if you have to. Once you start the ride, you must finish it.

He waited for the old dog to jump into the truck. The dog seemed happy just to sit next to him and eventually stretched out, taking most of the seat. He pulled into the same QuikMart that had mistakenly sold him the unwanted ticket. They were closed. He fished some change out of his front pocket. He bought another paper from the machine which was again a little damp by the time he got it in the truck. He opened to the lottery page. His eyes couldn't believe what they were seeing. The final number was a match. For a moment, he thought his heart had stopped beating. He couldn't swallow. Somehow, he managed to close the old truck door. Festus groaned at the inconvenience. It was the last thing Carlos recalled before pulling into his driveway.

He was home. Yes, it was his home. He felt safe here. Carlos took the lottery ticket and the receipt and folded them into the page of the newspaper with the winning numbers. He took a pen and in shaky handwriting wrote: Mr. George Wynn across the top of the page. He stuffed them into an envelope and quietly walked up to the big house. He shoved the envelope into the mail slot and took a deep breath. After all, it was Mr. G.'s ticket.

Lipstick Chronicles

"Irma, what time is my last interview?"

"Three o'clock, Ms. Roché. A Dean Grabber, used to be a store manager for Tar—" The speakerphone always cut off my assistant's last syllable. I never know if it's her quickness on the button or a malfunction of the system.

"Thank you."

Since coming to Finelle Cosmetics as HR manager, I've done hundreds of interviews. Today, I'm looking for a sales supervisor. It's always been our philosophy to promote from within. However, that's not always possible and now I'm even interviewing two men for the position. There was a time when a man wouldn't apply, but with the economy and the equal opportunity commission breathing down my throat…there's no choice. I'd be considering all candidates, even testosterone-laden hairy-chested ones.

"Ms. Emery is here for her appoint—" comes my assistant's voice over the intercom.

"Send her in, Irma."

I stand and shake her hand—delicate handshake, looks like she belongs on a parade float in North Carolina. Blonde, tiny, pretty, and perfect. *Weak, she's probably weak.*

"Please, have a seat," I direct, pointing to the chair. *Is that gum in her mouth?* Honestly—surely not. I'll keep watching.

90

"Did you read the job description my assistant gave you?"

It had been our practice for applicants to come in early and go over a detailed job description. The directive saved us time and helped us gauge their ability to follow directions. Some applicants study the paper the entire time they wait. Some of them give it a cursory look. Some barely glance. It's a good tool.

She nods. "I did."

Wafts of Britney Spears' Fantasy perfume make their way to my nose. "Is that Fantasy? It's nice that Britney has a cheap product line since she's getting a little old to be up on stage shaking her booty for the Kmart crowd. So, you were a store manager for KinderClothes?"

"Yes, for two years." Deep chocolate eyes with lash extensions blink back in confirmation.

"Why did you leave?" My favorite question.

Ms. Emery shifts her weight. *Uncomfortable, Missy. Come on—you bleach your hair—what's a little lie?*

"The hours. I was working about fifty hours a week—three nights."

Plausible. Maybe. Could mean she has children? I'm not allowed to ask, though. Could mean she's a drinker and the late nights interfered with her social life.

"This position requires some travel. You'll visit stores at least once a month. More if a problem comes up."

"That's fine, I'll drive—right?" She shifts her weight almost imperceptibly to the opposite hip.

"Yes, you'll drive your car, and we'll pay you mileage." *So, if she's willing to be on the road—why wasn't she okay with working nights?*

"Sure. I just bought a Prius. I'm saving a lot on gas."

A Prius, don't tell me…she's one of those granola-eating, make-your-own-soap environmentalists. I bet she has no idea what it takes to get a product from research to the shelf. Oh well, not my problem. "We need someone who can make sure the stores are keeping our products stocked properly, that every salesperson is trained in use and storage and that they are up on sales techniques for each product and every product line and that our lines are properly displayed. So, we are looking for someone with good people skills and a good eye." I'd memorized my lines. I could practically conduct an interview in my sleep.

"I did all of the displays for KinderClothes and the initial interviews for all hires."

Now her eyes seem wider. A sign of the truth. "Good," I say. "And inventory was probably handled from the district or home office?"

"Yes. But the selling was up to us!"

"Because most of our salespeople—" *not saleswoman I reminded myself—* "work for several companies and are actually store employees; we have to stay on top of it. If someone steals inventory, we might be out of a product for a while before it shows up on the computer records."

"Shrinkage is something I've been trained to prevent."

Kudos, Miss Sweet Potato Queen. We chat a few more minutes. I don't think she is tough enough for the cosmetic business. Clothes sell themselves, but you have to push lipstick. Wear it, breathe it and promise it will increase libido—I just don't think she has the chops for make-up. Still no sign of chewing gum. I thank her and she leaves.

My next victim reminds me of a chunky Dorothy Hamill— about forty, energetic, but ordinary. Not pretty, not unattractive, short plain hair. She sits down in the chair with a plop, making her seem larger than she is. "How long were you in sales?" I ask, not wishing to do the math.

"Fourteen years in cosmetic sales," she says. "Ten at Neiman's and four at Nordstrom's."

So, she knows cosmetics. Probably has to. Underneath the small rectangular glasses are the tiniest, beadiest eyes I've ever seen. But for mascara and lip gloss, the poor woman and her orthodontically challenged overbite would probably never get laid. And those hands, I've seen smaller ones on a Macy's balloon float. "Is travel an issue?" I say, pointing to the job description in her large hands.

"Oh, no. Travel's good. I like to drive. My partner and I drive everywhere."

Partner, ugh? *Crap...first a beauty queen now a lesbian.* "So, you probably know, Shannon, our last sales manager and you're familiar with our line?"

"Oh, yeah. I knew Shannon from Neiman's."

"That's right! She was head of cosmetics there before coming to work for us." *Finelle's first lesbian.*

"Shannon was great! That's what made me want to apply for this job."

Okay, Shannon was a bitch...but a tall, slender, sexy bitch with legs as long as toll roads. Is that how she knows Shannon? Testing our lipstick to its absolute limits! "Shannon's a piece of work. I know she can be a handful." *I really can't help myself.*

We spoke about the challenges of competing lines in a single store and I was impressed with her hands-on experience. But the actual hands. I couldn't quite get past the huge hands.... Next.

My ten o'clock interviewee had worked for a jewelry company. Laird looks promising, despite being gender-challenged for the cosmetic business. He is well-dressed: slim-fit designer shirt, dark trousers—no pleats. *Is that soap I smell?* He also has the greatest skin I've ever seen on a man. Dark blond hair combed to the side. A respectable length, but a fashionable one that sets off Prussian blue eyes. He could sell me lipstick any time. He sits across the desk and smiles.

"Laird, you think you might be interested in the wild, wild world of lips and lashes?" I like the way one side of his upper lip creeps up just slightly higher than the other one to reveal straight, but not too-perfect, white teeth.

"Sure, I like sales. Especially sales to women."

"I guess you know your way around a lipstick stain."

"Maybe," he says, appearing embarrassed.

He is likeable, but I'm surprised he did so well in jewelry—that blushing brides didn't decide they were getting the short end of the stick after meeting him. I want to crawl across my desk and unbutton his shirt. I won't because that would be wrong. He might be too hot for a cosmetics sales supervisor, but I have to be fair. I'll just tuck him away in the back of my mind—for later—when I have some time...alone.

My next prospect is younger. Although she is only 25, she has already owned and sold a small medical supply company. I look at her seated across from me. She appears as if she's in middle school—too small for the chair. I want to peek over and see if her feet touch the floor, even though it's not a job requirement. "Why are you interested in this job?"

"Well, I realized that one of my deficiencies is in sales. I think I had a handle on everything else in my own company, but I want to learn more about sales."

An honest answer. I like honesty. Her dyed hair is a little punked out, but we're a happening company. And how many ear piercings do I see? But hey, she has a lot on the ball. "You did your own hiring?"

"We did. My business partner and I shared interviewing."

Another partner. "So where did your 'partner' go?" I use air quotes for the word partner.

"He's still there. He bought me out."

"So he owns it 100% now?"

"He does. He had planned to buy me out from the beginning after he was trained and I was ready to move on."

"How come?"

"I started this company when I was nineteen. I was ready to try something else."

94

I notice she has on some make-up, but not a lot. Despite her age and her pixie demeanor, she seems competent—neat, tidy. Her answers show that she is well-spoken.

"So, do you know anything about cosmetics in general?" I say.

"Well, my mom wears make-up. So, I grew up looking through her stuff."

Not exactly the answer I'd hoped for. Maybe, "I'm familiar with department store marketing platforms," or "I like the new silicone-based formulas." But, "my mom wears make-up?" *How nice for her!*

"Well, it's a good thing you weren't an orphan. Thank you for coming in. We'll be making a decision next week." I stand, signaling her that the interview is over.

I sit in the beige, run-of-the-mill, office chair that has been my home for over a year. I cross my legs, which are outfitted in dark designer slacks meant to hide the five pounds I gained since leaving sales myself. I lean over my fake granite desktop and fold my hands. My salmon silk shirt sleeves tug on the front of my arms, resisting my urge to slump. I mull over the morning so far: I interviewed Miss Sweet Potato, Big Hands, Mr. GQ and the Business Barbie wannabe. Surely, the afternoon will get better. Maybe a full stomach will help. I always feel better after some Cheesecake Factory action.

~~~

"Okay, Irma. Please ask Ms. Wynn to come in."

"Ms. Roché, Don't forget Mr. Lange will be here on Friday for your annual performance rev—"

"Thank you, Irma." Just what I need, an uptight suit dogging my ass.

Ms. Wynn has a nice firm handshake. "Thank you for coming in," I say. Ms. Wynn is dressed professionally—always a bonus. Her blonde hair is a little dark at the roots, but it's cute and she's thin with high cheekbones, full lips and a straight nose—not like Paris Hilton, but straight.

"You have been a sales manager before, I see."

"Yes. I did outside sales for a linen supply company."

"So what did that entail?"

"I hired the sales associates and went with them on calls for training and reviews once a year. Or if something came up, I might have to fill in and make their calls for them."

"So you did commercial sales?"

"Yes, we also had a cloth diaper service and sometimes I did direct sales to people with babies if I needed to."

"Oh, I didn't even know anyone did that. That's great." This chick is sharp.

"The real profit is in the napkin and towel service."

"I can see that, you made good money," I say nodding to the resume in my hand. *But what did I just see? An Adam's apple? And the hands...again with the hands. This is a guy.* But the lipstick. It's perfect. Timber—our best shade. Good for blondes who don't want bright lips—subtle and disarming—when you don't want your lipstick to speak before you do. *Damn, damn, damn. I found the perfect sales manager. Except she's a he or was once a he. Do I want to be known as the HR manager who hires gender benders? Why didn't I become an optometrist like my mother wanted?*

"You do realize that most of our staff and clients are women?"

As Ms. Wynn leaves, I push the intercom button. "Irma, could you please ask Miss Sweet Potato to come back in tomorrow?"

"Miss who?"

"Um...Ms. Emery," I said shuffling through the applications.

~~~

"Irma, could you come in here?"

The heavy office door opens. "Did you need something Ms. Roché?"

"Irma, did we put an ad in the Times-Tribune?"

The slightly-graying middle-aged woman looks at me through rectangular DKNY glasses. "Yes ma'am we did," she says in stark monotone.

"Where else?"

"Jobsdotcom, our own website, the listserve, the local employment office." She ticked off the places on an imaginary list.

"I want to see the ad. The candidates we've had look like the cast of Rocky Horror."

"Just give me a moment." Irma disappears through the doorway, padding on the drab commercial carpet.

I take the opportunity to tuck my gray pinstriped shirt into my slacks a little deeper. Irma returns a few minutes later with a hard copy of the employment listing. I stare at the page with the sparse words: Sales manager for major cosmetics company. Experience in management. Must have own vehicle. $60K. Email resume to Irmap@finelle.com. *Damn. Why do I have to do everything myself?* "Why is this ad drawing such a freak show?" I look at Irma for answers.

She throws up her hands to the level of her shoulders. "I don't know that it's the ad. That's just what people are like nowadays."

"I feel like I'm auditioning actors for the audience scene in 'The Hunger Games.' Have you responded to every inquiry?"

"Almost." Irma shrugs. "A few just didn't have any experience."

"Let me see the emails and resumes. Now. Even if they don't have any experience, I'd rather find someone with a good work ethic and train them, than hire someone who looks like they belong in a circus."

"Yes, ma'am," Irma says, leaving the room, closing the door behind her.

A file lands in my in-box minutes later. *There are at least ten candidates here I didn't interview.* Irma is not exactly on her toes. *Did she even review these?* Probably just filled my appointment calendar and quit looking. People just don't give a shit anymore…anything to get by. Here's one: Shannon Carter. She worked as a nurse; used to sell Avon. I raise my voice, "Irma, please contact Shannon Carter and see if you can schedule her for an interview."

"You know she doesn't have any management experience." Irma's voice raises and cracks in frustration through the closed door.

I push the intercom button. "Have you ever even been in a doctor's office or a hospital? That's all they do—manage people."

"I meant sales manage—" Irma's voice springs out from the phone's speaker.

"Every time they give a shot or draw blood, they're selling. Convincing some poor sick sucker that 'this'll feel like a pinch,' when you know it's going to hurt like hell."

"Yes, ma'—"

"And Irma, what's wrong with this guy who sold auto parts?"

"Just didn't seem like a good—"

"No one just pops out of the womb selling lip plumpers! And what about Miss Sweet Potato?"

"I'm sorry, what did you—?"

"That first one, the blonde, what was her name? The one I asked you to contact yesterday."

"Emery. Constance Em—"

"Get her back in here. Mr. Lange is going to think we don't do anything around here."

"Yes, ma'—"

"Irma, you can send—let see, what's her name?—Ms. Carter…in."

I stand and greet the nurse. She's larger than most of the other candidates, but her make-up is—heavy, but flawlessly applied. "Good morning. Have a seat." *Or maybe two.* I point to the chair.

"I see here that you used to sell Avon. Did you enjoy that?"

"I did, but they put me on the noon to midnight shift at the hospital and that's when most of my Avon customers were home, so I stopped."

"Well, why do you want to change jobs—really it's professions?"

"Hospital nurses work twelve-hour shifts. It is just too long. By the time I get home, I'm completely exhausted."

Crap. She's tired. We're all tired. "We need someone who can make sure the stores are keeping our products stocked properly; that every salesperson is trained in use and storage and that they are up on sales techniques for each product and each product line and that our lines are properly displayed. So, we are looking for someone with good people skills and a good eye." Thank God, my spiel was over. "Do you have any questions?"

"When can I start?"

Not until you can pry your big butt out of that chair. "We are going to be conducting interviews through next week and then select candidates for a second interview. My assistant will let you know."

She rambles a few more minutes, then says, "Thank you for interviewing me."

"Well thank you for coming in." *And you should look into gastric bypass if you want a job in the real world sitting on other people's furniture.*

"Irma?" I say over the intercom.

"Yes?"

"Any luck with Ms. Emery?"

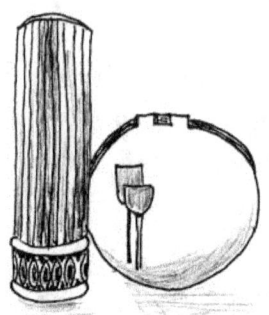

"No, but I'm try—"

"Have you tried texting her, or sending an e-mail?"

"Yes, both."

"When is my next interview?"

"Whenever he shows up. I emailed a schedule to—"

"I need one printed out and on my desk every morning. I don't always have time to log on and pull up my files. And Irma?"

"Yes?"

"Why are we out of coffee?"

"Yes ma'am. I'll make some…and ma'am… your next appointment is here and Mr. Lange called to confirm that he will be here on Fri—"

Of course he will be. "Send in my next prospect."

An average-looking Hispanic male walks in. He is nicely dressed: suit—check, tie—check. I shake his hand. "Hi, I'm Leslie Roché."

"Hi. Thank you for seeing me."

"Nice to meet you, Simon. Have a seat."

"I can see here that you have been in automotive sales and then you were a parts salesman for Pep Boys."

"I'm still at Pep Boys."

"So, why do you want to change jobs?"

He takes a deep breath. "I am not making much at Pep Boys. I like the work—I'm sort of into cars." He holds up dinged hands, palms out and leans forward a little in the chair.

I can see that the ridges and grooves in them are black with grease. "Have you considered digging ditches? Landscaping perhaps? Why did you quit automotive sales?"

100

"You know, I knew too much about cars to sell them. We had some cars that I knew were lemons. I can tell by the way something sounds if it needs a valve job or a new catalytic converter. I just couldn't stand by and let people buy something that was crap."

Honesty? How refreshing! But how would he feel about selling wrinkle serum? No one actually expects it to cure wrinkles—or do they?

"Simon, I like your attitude," I say, smiling. "We have a few more interviews to conduct and my assistant will be calling people next week. Thank you for coming in."

Then he was gone. As soon as the door to the outer office closed, Irma came in with a copy of my appointment schedule. "Ms. Roché, how was he?"

"He's a nice guy. Motivated, honest. I'm just afraid he might not be the one to train salespeople to push cosmetics…. Have you reached Ms. Emery by any chance?"

"Oh, yes. I got hold of her and she's not interested."

"Not interested? Did she say why? Did she get another job? Maybe I should talk to her—I have some leeway with the salary."

"I just really don't think she's into it."

"Irma, when you talk to these people, you have to sound upbeat. Like we're a happening company. Like it's fun to work here. If you just go through the motions, blah, blah, blah, no one is gonna want a job here."

"I'll see what I can do."

~~~

"How's that sales supervisor position coming?" Mr. Lange asks on Friday morning in the Finelle lobby.

"I'm going to run an ad in one of the trades. Maybe we'll have better luck if we go old school." I follow him down the hallway.

"Come in the conference room. I have us set up in here, Ms. Roach."

Roach?

He opened the door to the large space. "We're doing things a little different this year. We're using a review panel to evaluate employees."

Sitting at the back of the table were Irma, Miss Sweet Potato and Business Barbie.

Oh shit.

Mittens, Mama and Mashed Potatoes

It was the baby's first Christmas, the holiday that sets in motion subsequent memories that last a lifetime. The one grandmothers and great-grandmothers would talk about amongst themselves at graduations, weddings, and funerals for years to come. Relatives would come from near and far to see the first child born to the first grandchild. They'd speculate on what eye color she would eventually have, whether she would be tall or pretty, or smart or fair....

"My mother wants us to come for Christmas," the young wife said.

"What for? It's not like they haven't seen us in ages."

"Because it's Emma's first Christmas. Everyone wants to see her."

"Why?" the clueless neophyte chimed.

"Because they do!" invoked the wife with a careful mix of irritation and desperation in her voice. *How can it be that he just doesn't get it? That grandchildren have the ability to bring out the best in people—especially new grandchildren.* That for once, your mother isn't harping about your lack of make-up or your penchant for striped sofas...that she is so consumed with the little princess that you have brought into the world that she doesn't have the mental capacity to ask you when the last time you defrosted your freezer or cleaned under your oven.

"What about my parents? Do they have this same fascination?"

"Probably. It's why my mother invited them also."

"Let me get this straight. The people who didn't have time to take my phone calls when I was away at college and sick with pneumonia, the man who let me go an entire winter freezing to death because I lost my coat, the woman who asked me to spend my whole Christmas holiday planting oleanders—"

"Want to fly across the country in bad weather to spend Christmas with her first grandchild. Yes, we are talking about the same people."

"As long as I don't have to fly with them," the neophyte concludes.

"We'll take the cat," the wife decides. "That way we won't have to worry if the weather gets bad and we can't make it back on a certain day."

"You, me, Emma and Mittens in a Mini Cooper." The husband shakes his head, reliving the day he was talked into buying a car the size of an M&M.

~~~

On Christmas Day, everyone gathered at grandma's house—in-laws, friends, relatives and an Irish terrier mix named Harry.

"I'm a little nervous," the wife laments. I told Mom Emma was fussy, she said I didn't burp her enough. Then she said I shouldn't have let her sleep in the car for the whole trip. I wonder if your mother also thinks I'm a bad mother?"

"Emma is six months old. If you were a bad mother, she wouldn't have made it past six weeks."

"Thank you, Dr. Spock. I'll use that as my defense to Child Protective Services."

"It's going to be fine. What could go wrong?"

104

The wife hoists the car seat with the baby off the floor. "Let's go. Everyone is waiting. Can you get Mittens? I don't want her here on Mom's furniture unsupervised."

~~~

"Why, she looks like her mother," Aunt Grace whines loudly from the parlor sofa.

"But her eyes are a dark blue. Dark blue always means they'll turn brown," said the great grandmother. "How's the cat taking all of this?"

"Mittens is a little upset about having less lap time. But so far, no problems."

"How long have you had that cat?" the great uncle inquired. "Seems like a long time."

"About five years," the new mother commented.

"Gotta watch them cats," the uncle continued, "they'll suck the breath out of a baby."

"Goodness Clarence! That's just an old wives tale," Aunt Grace discounted. "Everyone knows that they smother babies because they are jealous. You don't let it near the baby when she's asleep? Do you?"

The new mother took the opportunity to leave the room before she had to answer any more questions.

Conversations drifted to politics, car models and the benefits of pulling ones' own teeth. A few helpful hints were proposed for anyone interested in venturing deep into the saliva pool.

Someone had bought into penny stocks, another had invested in an enchilada-on-a-stick franchise. No one liked the current president, and the cost of eyeglasses had become more expensive than anyone could bear. All in all, a pretty lively bunch.

Finally, the turkey was carved, the potatoes mashed and the relish dish staged. The buffet table loaded, it was time to eat. Just as some brave cousin was saying the "Amen" after grace, Harry the dog decided to make a move when he spotted the curious cat

creeping in to investigate the holiday feast. The cat, already out of sorts over the whole ordeal, jumped to safety when the dog lunged toward it. Unfortunately, the nearest refuge was the fully loaded buffet table.

The dog, undeterred by the difficulty of indoor hunting, began to bark and rose up on his hind legs in order to get a clear view of his lithe prey which frightened Mittens even more, causing her to embark on an escape path down the buffet table through the mashed potatoes, across the turkey, disturbing the cranberries and disrupting a pickle or two. By the time the cat had jumped to the nearest sanctuary—the kitchen, the whole room gasped in horror. Small spots of gravy had followed the feline from one end of the table to the other and then skipped over to the kitchen counter where the disturbed kitty was perched on the sink divider.

A stunned silence followed. No one knew what to say or do. Even pizza places were closed on Christmas day. They all stood and stared at the ruined Christmas dinner and the telltale gravy trail. After what seemed an eternity, the new father stepped up, lifted an empty plate from the pile and began to fill it.

"Well, I guess I'll go first."

The baby's mother followed. Before long, everyone was laughing and filling their plates; the baby sucked on a bottle while the cat sat licking the gravy from its paws.

Summer Psychology

It was May. I only needed one more class to graduate. College works like that. Your own schedule doesn't always jive with the university's. Experimental Psychology was only available every other spring semester. So, either I could wait until next spring or take the class somewhere else. Since I lived in a town with two major universities, I looked at the summer schedule for the other school. Bingo! Experimental Psychology, first summer session taught by a PhD whose name I recognized. I was only six weeks away from completing the requirements for my bachelor's of science degree. Happy dance…happy dance!

If only it had been that easy.

The first day was a parking nightmare. Fortunately, I'm a runner, so the mile I had to travel after I parked was only an inconvenience, not a deal breaker. My spirits brightened when I saw a couple of familiar faces in the sparsely populated classroom. Eventually, the other seats were filled by late students who were probably not tri-athletes. Out of breath, hot and sweaty, we all waited for our late professor. And it was worth it.

Professor Erudite was handsome and charismatic. He asked each of us how we came to take his class during the summer. My two compadres and I admitted that it was the fault of our all-female university that we were there.

Professor Erudite was elated, "You women come over here and kick our butts. Every time I've had one of you as a student, I was impressed." He turned away from us and spoke to the rest of the class. "Really, these three girls are going to make the best grades in this class. I don't know what they do over there," he pointed out the window, "but they will all get As. Mark my word."

Okay. No pressure here. But the class was interesting, and yes, I felt prepared. Part of the class was a lab. Twice a week we went to a lab class taught by a doctoral candidate. In that class, we crunched numbers. Everything we learned in the core class we wrote about in the lab. David, the doctoral candidate, kept us busy doing research and running formulas. He was determined to not be a pushover. Every week we had a new assignment, and every week we wrote a professional journal article. But he was also fun. I got to know him in the library where I spent most of my time.

He was preparing for his dissertation exam while I was trying to pass his class. Every day, I would see his balding head buried in a book and stop to say "hi." I liked him. He was a disenchanted Jew with a strong mind and a quit wit. We told jokes and exchanged stories. I enjoyed hearing him talk, but not for too long…I had work to do.

The six weeks seemed to fly by. I was surprised when Professor Erudite announced the schedule for finals. Only one more lab before the last exam. David said he was not giving us a final. He said that we had worked hard enough. I thought maybe he was just too exhausted to grade them. He had decided that we would have a competition instead. Boys against girls. He would give us the numbers and the name of the statistical instrument and we would write the formula and do the math on the board. Me and my homies were gonna have to bring it. And we did.

We were one point ahead going into the last round and I was up at the chalkboard. As soon as he read off the numbers, I was off and running. I ticked up the formula and plugged in the values. I was doing the math and looked over and saw that my competition was one decimal ahead. I poured on the steam and rounded up to finish the equation. Chalk dust was everywhere and my team was screaming as I wrote down the last numeral. In a moment of excitement, I tossed the eraser over my shoulder and did a victory leap. Unfortunately, I turned around to quiet shock. David had approached me without realizing the danger.

I stood there staring. He was frozen in his tracks and covered with chalk dust. His baldhead had the pattern of the square eraser and his eyebrows were white as snow. I immediately began to apologize for my lack of decorum, but to no avail. He was livid. Some of the students were doubled over laughing. I tried not to be one of them.

"I should have known you'd do something like this!" he yelled.

"I'm so sorry," I said again. "I had no idea…I just got caught up . . ."

By then his face and head were beet red. His eyes bulged out as he screamed. "Get out!"

So, I left. Humiliated. Stupidly, I retreated. I wanted to cry, but I didn't because I was too old to cry. I wanted to laugh because it was so damned funny, but I was too humiliated to laugh. *Shouldn't a real psychologist appreciate spontaneity?*

I went home and called Professor Erudite and asked him if I could take the final at another time, perhaps when he was giving one to a different class. I didn't tell him that I was a coward, that I didn't want to face my fellow students. I told him that I wanted to leave town as early as possible to go home, which was a six-hour drive. He was fine with it.

I slipped in and took the test early the next morning and was on the road by noon. I had several hours to think about David, his demons and the pressure he must've had capped inside his shiny head and thick glasses. I thought about how we all do stupid things.

Many years later, I was blessed with a precocious daughter. One day, I asked her to retrieve my purse from inside my locked car. Forgetting the car keys did not slow down her ten-year-old's

110

determination. She improvised and tried to pick the driver's door with a stick. Needless to say, her skills were not as adept as she estimated. The stick was broken off in the lock. I called around and found out a new lock would cost me two hundred dollars.

I didn't yell or lose my temper. I just reminded her that we were fortunate enough to be able to afford the repair and laughed it off.

When I think about the eraser foul, I can appreciate the abandonment of youthful enthusiasm and the weight of failure.

And how it had changed me.

Fortune in the Fountain

I've been a New York cop for almost a decade. I work in Manhattan where the Upper East Side meets Harlem, where have meets want. Some days I answer burglary calls about missing microwaves and computers; other days are about parking disputes and fender benders to high-end vehicles. Much of my time is spent on foot, so I get to experience law-breaking on New York streets firsthand—not at all like TV crime shows. I see poverty and drugs. I also see designer suits, lattes and joggers. Mainly, I see people just trying to earn a living and feed their families. But I'd never been tempted to arrest an eight-year-old, which is what makes this story so interesting . . .

     I first spotted the small black boy when he almost fell lowering his hand into a dormant public fountain under the watchful eye of the massive bronze angel above. When his arm emerged—sleeve wet, fist clenched—I knew he had scooped up a handful of coins, which is illegal, according to city statute.

The only reason I'd ever seen children that young steal was on impulse. Kids see something they want and they take it. But it was December and the city turns the fountains off in the winter. The stagnant water in the fountain was frigid, almost freezing. If that kid was willing to stick his hand in there, the money was probably for something important. I decided to turn the other way like I had for the dozens of homeless who fish out the change at night.

Two weeks later, I saw the same boy. Skinny, dressed in worn clothes, a faded oversized hoodie over a sweatshirt and thinning tennis shoes, he sat on the same spot. Snow flurried about while most people tightened scarves and fastened coat buttons or headed inside. He sat there in the approaching gloom as the crowds retreated. Again, he plunged an arm down into the ice-cold water, pulled it out and jammed a fist full of coins into his jacket pocket and took off down the street. What was he going to do with the money? Give it to drug-addicted parents? Use it to buy cereal? Milk? I could've stopped him. Maybe prevented one more kid from growing up to be a criminal. But I didn't. Whatever that kid needed the money for, he was willing to risk hypothermia. I had to give him credit. I wouldn't reach into the cold nasty water for a handful of coins. Once, I'd arrested several boys for urinating in the same fountain. Seems to be a rite of passage for some of them. The memory just added to why I couldn't imagine anyone sticking their hand in there on a cold December day.

About a week later, I saw the kid go into a bodega about a block away. His nose was snotty and he had on the same threadbare sweatshirt I'd seen the week before. I followed.

"Three bananas, please," he said to the grocer just as I arrived.

Only three? And he said, "please." The kid took the bananas and paid with a bill. He immediately peeled one of the bananas and starting eating. I sensed his situation was not the best. He might even be homeless. The change would probably buy his dinner or his breakfast. I'd been a poor Italian kid in the Bronx whose parents worked long hours, I knew the drill.

Over the next two months, I spotted him several more times. Yeah, I felt for the kid, but how long was I supposed to look the other way? *Maybe I should do something.* Tell his parents—make that parent. Most of these kids are lucky to have one parent in the home. Or call Children and Family Services to investigate? I didn't have a name, an address—nothing. Who was I kidding? Why did I let this one kid get to me?

About a month after I saw him in the bodega, I noticed my little thief again and decided to follow him. Once more, he went to the fountain and scooped up the change left by poor hopefuls in need of a bit of luck. I hung back far enough to blend in with the crowd. The boy began walking down 110th. It was difficult to see his small form slipping in and out of the pedestrians, but maybe I could pin down the neighborhood or see a building number. Then I could ask around. He always had on the same clothes. Shouldn't be too hard to identify the skinny kid with the faded red sweatshirt, hole-ridden jeans and worn-out Vans.

He was about a half a block ahead. He caught the light and crossed over to the next block. I had to skirt traffic to keep up. Just what I needed. "New York flatfoot hit by delivery van," in tomorrow's *Times*. We moved toward one of the nicer blocks on my beat. Brownstones flanked by high-rises. There was more landscaping; planters dotted the easement between us. He entered the small quadrangle next to one of the high-rises. What was his business there? Those places go for over a million bucks. I stood outside and looked into the large, glassed-in lobby. The doorman let him in without incident and I saw the kid walk over to an elaborate fountain with a modernized bronze figure in a flowing

114

gown channeling water between braided hair that hung on either side of a featureless face.

He held out his hand and dumped the coins into the basin.

What the hell? This kid from Harlem was traveling over a mile to put change into a fountain located in one of the nicer parts of the city in the dead of winter? I shook my head. *Like I'm going to arrest an eight-year-old for money laundering?*

I headed back to my beat, hoping I hadn't been missed. I couldn't quite wrap my head around the whole strange event. Why would he think the doctors, lawyers and other professionals needed coins from my beat? And why did he deliver them? I thought about the boy and his pilfering every day for a week. It was starting to drive me a little crazy. The amount of change couldn't have come to more than a dollar. Even if the kid did it every day, it was barely a misdemeanor…but what if it wasn't the amount of money?…what if it was the value of the change?…and what if that value was luck?

Some people believe in it—not me—otherwise the money wouldn't be there in the first place. Actually, a lot of people must have faith in it. It's what drives lotteries, casinos and contests. But who would believe in it enough to stick their hand in ice-cold water and then walk over a mile?

How much luck does he need? And how long before he gets discouraged and moves on to more nefarious things, hoping for a windfall?

Funny thing, I couldn't get this kid out of my head. And why that fountain? Those people obviously had their share of luck. They live in some of the most expensive apartments in the city. The obsessive thoughts started to keep me awake at night.

I decided to use my day off to solve the mystery—a small price to pay for a good night's sleep. I put on gray corduroy pants, a warm jacket and a dark watch cap. Even though I'd never worked undercover, I knew that I didn't want to stand out. At nine-thirty, I walked to the high-rise with coffee and a paper and took a seat on a bench outside the building. Around noon, I saw the boy. He had on a jacket, but there was no mistaking his size and the sweatshirt hanging out below. I saw him go in, pull coins out of his coat pocket and drop them into the fountain. Then he took a seat next to me and waited. His fingers looked chapped and the coat sleeves had a line of stain about halfway up the elbow. He wiped away traces of a milk mustache with his sleeve like kids do.

I was tempted to ask him where he got the money and why he brought it here, but I didn't want him to know I'd been watching. It wasn't long before a thin black woman in a dark dress and large smile came out of the elevator. The boy stood and walked over as she exited the lobby. The woman, who shared his nose and chin, carried a bag and I suspected that she worked in the building as a maid or nanny since the boy didn't go up the elevator. She put her arm around him, he surrendered a slight hug and they left together. *So, his mother works here. A clue, but it still doesn't explain the coins.* Maybe he was just grateful his mother had a job. I could see a penny—maybe. But this kid was tenacious. He'd probably made thousands of wishes with all that change. What could possibly be so important?

I continued to obsess about the boy and his coins. Maybe he went back late at night and stole them when no one was looking—using the fountain as a holding bin. No, it would have been too easy to just keep walking when he had them in his possession. I had to go back. I wanted to know. I needed to know.

My next day off, I went to the building again. But it was a Saturday and I didn't know if the kid would show. I parked myself on the same bench about ten and pretended to be interested in my phone like every other New Yorker. Around eleven, the boy appeared and took a seat on a bench close by. *What the hell am I thinking? Why don't I just ask him?* Then the elevator door opened and the same woman came outside pushing a wheelchair. In it was a blonde boy about the same age as my thief, but frail and pale with blue eyes. The boy next to me jumped to his feet, his eyes lit

116

like firecrackers. A huge smile claimed his face. The two boys exchanged fist bumps. They launched into a conversation that had started long ago, both excited to see the other, both talking at once. I knew immediately what the change was about. The three left together, but I couldn't see where they went…I could no longer focus.

I pretended to be with an older couple and followed them into the building's lobby. Shuffling over to the fountain, I looked down. A brass plaque mounted to the fountain bore the words: "St. Serafina—Patron Saint of the Physically Challenged."

I stared at the build-up of coins for a moment…then tossed my own.

Drought

"I need some fresh air!" I shout, making my exit. The door slam is merely a fraction of the rage that I really feel. Only if the entire house had collapsed in ruins would it be commensurate to my emotions. *Damn him! Damn his ass! How did I get into this mess?* I march down my suburban street and head toward the trail that leads into the nearby mountains. It's a path I know well, unlike the man I am sharing my bed with.

The simple shoes I have on are not for hiking, however, the anger I feel is far more powerful than any discomfort the flats generate. I look ahead to the live oaks and the rail fence that welcomes hikers to the national recreation area. Ample rainfall has invited all manner of plants and animals to proliferate this year. The gnarled giant oaks are weighty with leaves, and numerous juvenile rabbits skitter about, unsure of my presence or intentions.

I plod along the dirt path until the fence ends and I am alone with the scrub and the yucca tucked in amongst the tall needle grass. The Santa Monica Mountains have a roughness to them. Even in the foothills, there are rocky fortresses and endless cacti, and if I didn't count the prick I live with, the California blackberry is one of the thorniest fruits around. *How could I have found yet another rat of a man?*

The air is clean except for a hint of the earthy smell and the humidity that remains a day or so after a rainfall. The dust is gone, the plants have clean shiny faces and even though the sun is also

118

shining, my spirits are dim. Each step I tread takes me further and further from the lies I want to believe. A small incline leaves me breathless, much like the sex we once had. At the top of the hill, I can see into the backyards of the homes below—swing sets, swimming pools and spoiled pets. I have to wonder if the men in those homes are liars…are their lives a vile concoction of what we want people to think and what really is?

The downhill grade is more treacherous than the uphill side. Here there are loose rocks and furtive wet, slippery spots. The shoes are not practical for the difficult terrain—my feet slide around inside them. I need hiking boots, something sturdier, with more support. I look around at the clear blue sky that Californians worship. If only my life could be as clear as the sky. But, I have to remind myself that it was just yesterday that it rained and buckets of water tossed out by the heavens changed the entire landscape. People stayed home while sirens wailed, speeding to countless fender benders on slick, flooded city streets.

The newness after a rain always promises hope, perking up the wildflowers that must have a difficult time in this area— drought one part of the year, mudslides the other. Yet, they survive. Some small, tiny part of their glorious regalia always perseveres to re-sow again, coming back stronger and more beautiful than before. The plants on either side of the trail ahead are known as nightshade. The sweet purple flowers belie the evergreen shrub's potential. All parts of the plant are known to be poisonous. The Italians call it "belladonna"; it means "beautiful woman." The wives of Emperor Augustus and Claudius both found it useful for eliminating enemies and here it is, just waiting to be picked. The ingestion of a single leaf can be fatal. Nature cares for its own.

The sun is warming my head and while my breathing increases, a strange calm brings comfort.

Before long the moisture-less summer will roast the leaves and burn the flowers…then all we can do is be patient, waiting again for the rain and the hope they bring.

Legend of the Blue Morphos

"Earth Mother, Earth Mother, where are you? We must speak. I have some very important news from the tribunal." The girl spoke in urgent tones.

"What say you, my dear? You know this is my busy season." The voice rang out clear as a bell.

"I have been selected to attend the spring formal in the meadow," the girl answered.

"I am very happy for you, but there will be no spring if I'm not allowed to finish my work."

"But the tribunal says that you will find me an escort and that only you can dress me for such an occasion."

"Those old hags? They have been dogging me for eons. First, it was too much rain, then not enough rain. After that, it was too cold. Then I engineered global warming and now it's too hot. You'd be better off in a different dimension. This one needs another large asteroid."

"But I like it here," the smaller voice asserted. "There are trees and flowers, brooks and birds. I think it's beautiful."

"Yeah, yeah, yeah. There are also the Kardashians, and by the way, I thought I got Bruce Jenner's Adam's apple just right the first time. And in case you haven't heard, there is a drought happening in North America. I can't make humans happy. What a bunch of crybabies. I'd like to see a human take over my job. The first time one of them had to work overtime, it would be "Katie, bar the door." People are all about recreation, shopping and entertainment. When was the last time I got a day off?"

"Well, I don't really know. I heard on the edge of the forest that the 1960s were pretty laid back." The girl looked down, ashamed that she'd listened to gossip.

"I'll tell you who took that decade off—God!" I was busy. Have you ever heard of the blizzard of 1967? Chicago got 24 inches of snow in 29 hours. And how about the Lindsey storm? Twenty five inches of snow in New York and Boston."

"What was God doing?"

"I have no idea. He won't say. Someone said he had work done, but he didn't look any different to me when he finally returned. In fact, he never changes. The guy is amazing. He looks just like he did when I met him and what I wouldn't give for those cheekbones."

"So, I guess it's no on the dress?" the girl said, trying to rein in her counselor.

"Let me think about it. There is so much to choose from: the frosty white of a waterfall during spring thaw, the iridescent crystal of a morning dewdrop, the sun kissed yellow of a spring tulip, the orange head of an olive warbler, the pale petal pink of a Tuscan rose…. May I ponder this until the end of whaling season? I really do have all of my resources tied up right now. I never know what you people are going to do next."

"Certainly," the young girl replied. "The formal won't be until the last frost has passed."

"Damn! I forgot to schedule the last frost. Ta ta. See you soon." Earth Mother was off to save the world.

The girl did not hear from Earth Mother for many weeks. She looked in the forest, across the meadow and in the nearby foothills. She even called upon her winged friends to search the desert sands, but still no sighting of the Earth Mother. Meantime in the meadow, the flowers were awakening, the bugs were buzzing and whispers about the last frost abounded. It was the next

122

morning when the girl went to the meadow. Her feet crunched the frozen grasses. The field was quiet as the sun peeked over the forest. "I guess she got around to the last frost," the girl said to herself in the still crispness. "Now if only she has time for me."

Within days, the once-quiet meadow began to burst with activity. Gold Contra Costas leapt toward the sky, bees hummed and birds danced in the trees. The spring formal would be soon. Still there was no news from Earth Mother. The girl walked to the brook and looked in the water for a sign, but the cool, swollen stream just stared back and said, "She's been here, but I don't know where she is now."

The girl climbed a tree to ask a bird if she'd seen Earth Mother. The bird said her eggs were set so she knew Earth Mother had been there, but the young starling had no idea where she'd gone. The girl finally went to the middle of the meadow, laid down and shouted at the sky, "Where art thou? I too am your child. Am I not worthy?" The sky only clouded up and delivered a short spring rain in reply.

The next day, the girl could smell the freshness of new grass. It was the day of the much anticipated event. All of the flowers were wearing the latest sepals. Still there was no word from Earth Mother. The girl cried her blue eyes dry. How could her own mother have forgotten her? The rabbits began to assemble, and whippoorwills began to sing. Spring could not wait. The girl hid so no one would know that Earth Mother had forgotten her precious daughter.

On the edge of the forest, the girl looked over the busy procession. Then, she hung her head, leaned on the nearest alder and closed her eyes in shame. While stoically accepting her fate, small prickly sensations enveloped her body. She tingled from her shoulders to her toes. The only other time she'd ever felt this way was when she was almost struck by lightning during a thunderstorm in the forest. *Is it happening again? Am I to die?*

Finally, when she couldn't stand still one more minute, she opened her eyes. What she saw was astonishing—a beautiful cerulean covered her body and flowed onto the ground. Thousands of blue butterflies had come to perch themselves upon her, forming the most exquisite dress the girl had ever seen. They tickled her breast, trailed over one shoulder and flowed down her back to rejoin their family at her waist. "Earth Mother! Earth Mother! Where are you? It's the most beautiful gown ever made!"

"I'm glad you like it, dear. I do some of my best work under pressure," the voice rang out again.

"Thank you! Thank you! It will be the prettiest dress in all the town."

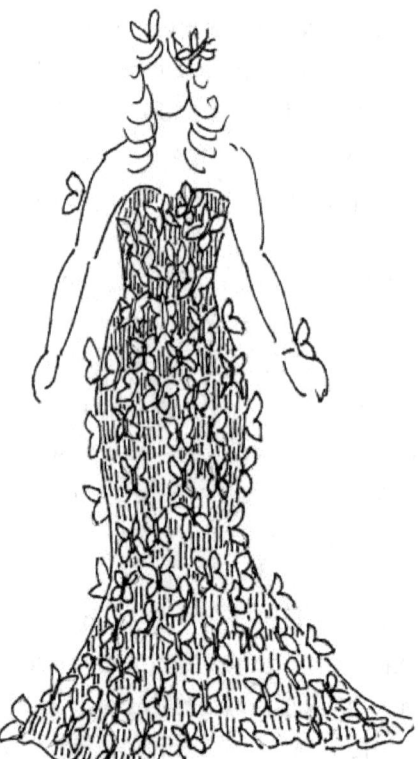

"You do have some stiff competition, but I like competing with myself—gives me something to shoot for."

"But I can't go alone…can I?"

"And you won't, my dear." Earth Mother nodded at the nearby alder whose smooth bark now sported a tuxedo made out of hundreds of black click beetles."

"He is very handsome, but can he dance?"

"Just for tonight."

"What can I do to repay you?" the girl inquired.

"You can have fun and be home by midnight so the blue morphos can continue on their journey and the click beetles can play at their evening gig."

"Really, that's it? Just so I understand—the butterflies leave at midnight?"

"It is so, my dear."

"Thank you, again."

The ball was even grander than the girl had imagined. Spring was wearing its most sublime finery. She had never seen so many colors and shapes in her whole life. Spidery witch hazels, demure bluets and ruffly purple hellebores all swayed in the breeze. When she was introduced to the meadow dwellers, they gasped as the wings of the butterflies waved in return. She danced, laughed and drank in the fragrant spring air. It was the most wonderful night of her life. And when it became late she laid again in the meadow and looked up at the moon and the stars and bid the butterflies adieu.

She awoke naked to the flutelike song of the meadowlark welcoming a new day from the nearby alder. As the dawn subsided, a blue sky appeared. It was the bluest of blues, bluer than any before. When she sat up, she saw a single butterfly flutter up into the sky higher and higher until it no longer was a butterfly, but a part of the most beautiful day in all the spring.

When the girl became a young woman, Earth Mother returned and spun her into a cerulean goddess and gave her dominion over all the meadow. But even though she was more beautiful than the night of the ball, she was still lonely because she had no one to talk to and she again called to Earth Mother for guidance. "Earth Mother, I know you have given me the grandest gift of all. So why am so lonely?"

"Think about it, dear. You have yearnings from your human ancestors. How many times has Christie Brinkley been married?"

"I don't know. Should I contact her?"

"Don't bother, instead return to the smooth bark alder and see if the answer to your problem is in your own back yard."

The goddess went to the alder, which was now tall and sturdy, and she knelt against its trunk and gently traced the bark with her fingertip. In a moment, the bark dropped away and a handsome prince remained standing next to the dewy goddess.

"Earth Mother, Earth Mother, he is very handsome. Is there any way I can thank you for such a wonderful gift?"

"My dear, it is quite enough that you have never asked for your own reality show! Be happy."

Moral of the story: No matter how spectacular the ball is, good girls should leave by midnight if they want a prince.

First Day...First Grade

I'd gone to kindergarten, but first grade was not the same. I wasn't a baby anymore. I would learn to read. The tables and the buckets where kindergartners stored crayons had been replaced with desks. The cheery walls had become dreary chalkboards. I sat on a metal chair with a lacquered wooden seat. My new dress let the backs of my thighs stick in place, which made movement awkward. The smiling nubile kindergarten teacher was gone. A small, thin-lipped woman in her sixties was in charge. Mrs. Coates had a bygone style with a tight gray bun at the nape of her neck.

This was progress. I was in a real school with big kids. When I was younger, I'd longed to learn to read and had

asked to be taught on many occasions. No one seemed to have the time. My books were held hostage by adults who doled out the magic of the words when they saw fit. I wanted the code, the knowledge that unlocked adventures and other worlds. School was the place where this would happen. The older, matronly teacher was my passport to freedom.

The morning was filled with roll call, lunch money collection and instructions on things like how to behave and what was expected of us big kids. We could only speak if we raised our hands and were called upon to do so. Tattling would not be tolerated. Books were only allowed on our desks when we were told to take them out. Bathroom breaks were given twice a day. No other potty times were allowed. There was a stool in the corner for anyone who misbehaved. The class was finally given a milk break where everyone learned to manage a milk mustache in front of strangers. Some of us quickly wiped it away; others smiled and enjoyed the attention.

A photographer from the newspaper came in and took pictures for the annual "Back to School" edition. The day that makes mothers breathe a sigh of relief and fathers hopeful that they will have sex again. A photo of me sporting my pixie haircut was in the next day's newspaper with the caption, "Shelly Johnson, son of Mr. and Mrs. Herman Johnson." The pixie was my mother's answer to the school day hair dilemma. I came to hate that picture...and, as many people do—all the ones that followed.

Lunch in a real cafeteria was noisy. Teachers shushed while forks clanged and plastic trays collided. Some kids brought food packed by caring mothers who poured heated soups into thermoses and constructed sandwiches packed in colorful lunchboxes— mothers who did not rely on short haircuts.

After lunch we went back to the classroom for a few minutes before we were dismissed for recess. Just as the bell rang for the most important part of the day, Mrs. Coates walked up to the front of my desk and pointed a crooked finger at the boy next to me.

In a voice I'd only heard from broomstick pilots, she said, "Young man, you will stay here. Right here! I am not putting up with your nonsense," she cackled. The finger moved as the hand shook with anger.

Until that moment, I hadn't noticed the boy next to me. He had a buzz hair cut. Like my hair cut, it said, "Low maintenance, owner too wiggly for daily styling." He was a little bigger than most of us. He'd seen the inside of a first grade classroom before.

The rest of us went to recess—the fate of the boy with the short hair unknown. Some kids played on playground equipment. The "athletic kids" were dressed in shorts or jeans and tennis shoes and began to cross the monkey bars and climb up ropes. The remaining girls stood and talked, pulled down our dresses in the wind to hide our underwear and envied the kids in jeans and shorts. We waited for another bell to ring—the one that would bring us in and change our attitude about school, but we didn't know that and we waited to be summoned.

We entered the cool classroom to find the boy with short hair crying, his face apple red, his eyes swollen and teary. Our teacher stood behind her desk where a large wooden paddle rested on its surface. No one said a word. The boy buried his head in crossed arms on his desk. I felt sorry for him. I'd not seen him do anything wrong, not utter a sound. His sins were a mystery to me. Worse than that, the tiny woman had brought the big boy to tears. No telling what she could do to someone my size. I wanted to run away, escape, go someplace safe where no one was allowed to hit me. I no longer wanted to read.

The teacher never had any more problems with the big boy or with anyone else in that first grade classroom, and I came to find out, Dick and Jane were a pretty easy read. I never understood why words had been hidden from me for so long or why anyone needed a paddle to teach them.

Gambling on Motherhood

The Gambles only had one offspring—this year. In previous seasons, the two had been sighted with as many as five little ones. The mating pair of Gambles quail had been returning to our property for several years. This year there was only the small family, but the pair was no less proud. They paraded the little chick around the yard soon after it was hatched and then took a layover on my patio. The *cheeper* was barely two inches in height, but ready to chase bugs—and chase it could. The tiny bird was audaciously nimble. Able to balance on a single blade of grass; it traveled across the yard as if it were walking on water. Up and down, up and down, the little quail rode stray twigs and sailed aboard low-lying plant leaves. All the while, momma and papa raced to keep up. It was obvious that nature intended for two parents to raise these energetic babies.

The couple was particularly colorful this year. Older now, the male was an iridescent blue on the top half and both birds had a tall plume on their head that hung over and bobbed in front of their faces. They were a beautiful example of a species that thrives only in the Southwest United States. I always looked forward to their visits and the adventurous babies that kept them on their toes.

A few days later, I was working in the backyard and heard the ruckus of a loud, nasal ka-KAA-ka—then louder, more urgent, two simultaneous ka-KAA-kas. I walked over near the wall that separated me from my next door neighbors. The mother quail flew up and landed on top of the stone structure and continued her noisy rant. I could see the father about thirty feet away on the ground behind my house also fussing and I sensed their frantic anxiety. The female, now only about four feet from me, turned and stared straight into my eyes while she danced the frenetic jitter of desperation. I looked over the fence and what I saw distressed me also. A black and white cat slinked along the hill behind my house toward a shrub buried in the afternoon shade of an oak. For a second I froze. Quail will nest on the ground or in low-lying scrub. The baby had to be on the cat's lunch menu. In order to stop the hunter, I would have to go and bring back a step stool or ladder to scale the surrounding fence. Leaving would make the quail even more vulnerable. Instead, I did what any experienced animal control officer would have done: I yelled. "SHOO!" I yelled again and again . . .

The last time something like this happened, I had been returning to my parked car from the local grocery store the summer before. A young mother parked next to me was just about to get in her vehicle and leave when the door to her van rolled shut. She shouted as if in pain and began to beat on the closed door in the 85 degree heat. I went over and tried to find out what had happened, but quickly assessed by the woman's cries that there was a baby locked in the van.

I looked in to see a tow-headed toddler holding a key ring who was happy as a clam. "Do you have anyone with an extra key who you can call?" I asked. Through the sobs, I understood that she lived in the next county. "My mother-in-law will never forgive me. She already thinks I'm a bad mom!" she cried. More wails were emitted, and more sobs were born.

"Oh, all mothers make mistakes. I'll just call the fire department," I said.

"It's too hot! He'll die!" she shouted collapsing to the pavement.

"We'll watch him. If he looks red or like he can't breathe, I'll break in myself. It's going to be fine." I contemplated which window I would break to minimize any risk to the baby.

Fortunately, the fire truck rolled up in less than five minutes. The fireman spoke with the young mother and then came over to me. "Can you stay with her? Maybe over there. See if you can get her to calm down," he said. I walked the desperate mom to the sidewalk and held her while she cried and told her that all mothers do stupid things.

"The trick is to not tell your mother-in-law. I promise you that she made mistakes too. Time has just made the memory of her own parenting closer to perfect."

Within fifteen minutes the emergency responders had opened the locked van. I retrieved some thawing popsicles out of my groceries and gave one to both mother and son.

I understood both the young mother and the quail. One summer afternoon, my own three-year-old daughter slipped out of the garage while searching for the cat. Within a minute, I saw a car come to a stop in front of our house. I flew out the front door in a panic and found a strange man standing in our driveway talking to my toddler.

"I saw her pull on the cat's tail as I was driving by," the man said. "I work for animal control and most of the calls we get about bites are because a kid aggravated the animal."

Trying to pretend that I believed him and squelch my internal mom alarm, I assured him that our cat was quite tolerant. I wanted to write down his license plate, to call the police and see if his story was true, but mostly I wanted my heart to stop racing so I wouldn't have to kick the man in the groin and scream. Somehow I thanked him—really!—and went back into the house with my daughter and locked the doors. I definitely knew how the mother quail felt.

Back on the lawn, I continued to shoo the cat and my screams did not go unheeded. My neighbor came out and scolded the cat, taking it inside. The Gambles hurried back to check on their offspring.

I never saw the baby quail again, but occasionally the mother quail returns and drinks from my fountain while I'm in the yard and I like to think she knows that I too am a mother and…no one messes with our babies.

The Exhumation

I reached down and dug my manicured fingers into the mound of dirt to capture some of it in my palm. Not too much—I wasn't going to bury the urn single-handedly—it was purely symbolic. The dampness of the soil was cool in my hand. I tossed it toward the grave and brushed my hands together to rid them of any lingering traces.

When the funeral director had asked me what sort of service I wanted, my brain went blank. Nothing had come to mind except the ancient ritual of throwing soil. It seemed fitting. My mother already had the ashes to ashes part covered when she died of lung cancer after a lifetime of smoking and wished her body cremated. Carol Ann stood behind me and followed my lead. It was only right. I'd discovered only weeks before that she had given birth to me.

We walked toward the cars parked along the cemetery road. I felt as if I should say something, but I'd be damned if I knew what it was. Just a few days before, Carol Ann had been a much older cousin, one of only two. Today she is my biological mother. What is there to say? Yes, we do resemble one another. And yes, both of us love the color fuchsia—other than that, we're just two people who happened to come from the same peculiar gene pool. "I'm going to run home and change shoes," I said.

"Okay, I'll meet you at my folks' house," Carol Ann answered.

134

When I turned my head toward Carol Ann, I could see my aging aunt and uncle creeping along behind us. I had to wonder if I should think of them as my grandparents now—which technically, they are, but I never would have guessed.

I opened my car door and smiled in their direction. I could have rented a limousine, but I wasn't ready to share a car with the relatives. Especially since I wasn't certain about how I felt about being in close quarters with them. My whole world had changed. I guess I should be grateful. Carol Ann is a much better person than my mother had been.

~~~

I thought back a month prior to that day in the hospice. Mom was watching *Forensic Files* when I arrived. "I'm glad you're here. There's something I need to talk to you about," my mother had said in a thin, gravelly voice.

"Sure," I answered.

"Let's go outside so I can have a cigarette."

Some people quit smoking once they are diagnosed, but not my mother. It only reinforced her reason for smoking: "We're all goin' sometime."

I helped her boney frame into the wheelchair and grabbed her purse from under the small table by her bed. It was an ugly purse: too large, too full, too gaudy.

A tall man who was out on the patio smoking opened the door for us. Mother pulled out a pack of Winstons—her best and only friends—and stared at the cylindrical cohorts. She made chit chat about the view of the parking garage. Finally, the man left and she asked me if I'd spoken to my cousins, Carol Ann or Diana, lately.

I had to think for a second. "Yes, about a week ago." I wasn't close to my two cousins, but I was fond of their parents—my Aunt Linda and Uncle Leo—so it wasn't unheard of.

"I want you to know, we never planned to tell you. I wanted you to know, but I promised Linda I wouldn't."

"Okay…tell me what?"

She looked away, and turned toward the parking structure. "You know how your grandmother was…always worried about what the neighbors would think?"

I knew how Gran was. She'd never done anything wrong. Never lost her temper. Didn't drink, didn't smoke, probably never had sex out of wedlock. Her only vice was gossip. She didn't even spread much of that until her declining years, but she was a gifted listener. She eventually told me things I never wanted to know: like how Mama wouldn't hold me if I cried and how my grandfather wouldn't pay for Mama's college after she married. Why do people think as they approach death's door they have to tell everything they know?

"Well, you need to know that it was never my idea to deceive you. I wanted to tell you when you were four, but no one thought it was a good idea."

Nothing was ever my mother's fault. She was the quintessential victim. In fact, her death was the fault of Big Tobacco and she had a copy of the settlement to prove it.

"When your cousin Carol Ann went off to college, she got pregnant right off the bat. She came home for the Christmas holidays and her parents were beside themselves. Linda was just certain they would take away Leo's judgeship and she would lose her teaching job."

"Can they do that? It's not a crime, you know."

"It is in our family. Our mother was fit to be tied. She was ready to put the house up for sale and move across the country."

"Really?"

"So, your father and I decided to adopt you. Carol Ann took the next semester off and went to Leo's aunt's house to give birth and it saved us all the embarrassment of Carol Ann's whoring around."

136

Is this true? My birth was just the result of an indiscretion my family couldn't tolerate? My whole life I'd known I was a huge imposition to my parents, but I never thought it was because I was a bastard. I'd been told I had too much energy, that I made too much noise, that I annoyed everyone…I just thought it was because my parents were older. Shock froze my expression as I tried to assimilate the information. I didn't want to give my mother the satisfaction of a reaction one way or the other.

"Why didn't she just put me up for adoption?" *Why couldn't I have taken my chance with some clueless stranger who might have really wanted me?*

"Your aunt and uncle were afraid you'd find out who your mother was and then eventually they would have to deal with you all over again."

"So, why now?"

She leaned over and put the cigarette out in the ashtray on the nearby table. "Carol Ann thought you should know and I thought I should be the one to tell you. After all, it only takes one murder and DNA starts flying everywhere."

I stared at her in silence. *Your glass is completely empty, isn't it?*

"As far as I'm concerned, you are my daughter and you always will be. Carol Ann has always resented me and said I stole you. I can assure you everything was above board and she signed all the papers."

"What about my father? Do I have a father out there?"

"Well, I suppose you do. Somewhere. Carol Ann wouldn't say who the father was."

"Is. If he is alive, he IS my biological father."

Mama lit up another cigarette. "True, but your daddy loved you. Even if he did abandon us for that slut waitress."

Mama didn't live too long after this. I figured she'd probably just wanted to beat Carol Ann to the punch. And now, here I was at the funeral of one of the nastiest people I'd ever known while my biological mother hovered nearby.

I pulled up in front of the house my aunt and uncle had owned for almost forty years and took a deep breath before stepping out of the car. People would come a-calling and I would shake hands and thank them for their presence, all the time knowing that there wasn't a soul there who wasn't glad Mama was dead. There weren't too many people alive she hadn't offended or threatened to sue. In this part of the South, people came to pay their respects and it wasn't necessarily for the deceased. It was for the family, for the possibility of future real estate deals, the chance to schmooze, to admire the flowers, to see how much money was spent on the service, and to see what funeral goers were wearing.

I opened the old screen door and entered my uncle's home. The living room was crowded with dare I say "mourners." I could see the sacrificial ham sitting on the dining room table. Carol Ann looked younger than she had at the cemetery. My aunt and uncle were in the kitchen, moving the recent onslaught of dishes around. I didn't want to be there and I didn't want to make small talk. I

 headed over to a spot on the sofa and sunk down. With any luck, my dark blue dress would just blend in with the sofa's blue and no one would be the wiser. A few moments later, I saw Carol Ann head in my direction. "Sweetie, why don't you let me get you a plate? There are some casseroles or maybe you would just like a little salad and pasta?" Carol Ann laid her hand on my shoulder and looked at me with concern and it wasn't just polite concern. It was genuine fondness.

"This will probably go easier if you have some food in your stomach."

138

"Sure," I responded. "Anything's good." Carol Ann slipped through the crowd, disappearing into the kitchen.

It hadn't occurred to me that Carol Ann had mourned the loss of her child. I'd just assumed she was happy to be rid of me, but something in her eyes hinted at loss. She had never married. She was a librarian who'd encouraged hundreds of children to read. Had Carol Ann suffered as much as I had? Had she wanted a daughter as much as I had hoped for parents who loved me? The space between us closed as she brought a carefully filled plate in one hand and a glass of tea in the other.

I took the plate offered and the promise of love that came with it.

Scattered Ashes

Still holding the urn containing his father's ashes, Stephano flipped the open/closed sign around for the first time since Benito's death.

In twenty-three years, Benito's Bistro had never failed to open at four p.m.—not when floods stopped traffic on the lazy street, or on the holidays that his father had so loved. Nor had it closed before midnight. Benito's was a mainstay on the east side. Everyone knew Benny, his artichoke bruschetta, the shrimp ravioletti, and the whole grain pizza crust.

Stephano had grown up in the restaurant's kitchen. He learned to fill cannoli before he knew how to multiply. He could identify garlic types from across the room before his twelfth birthday. Stephano knew the restaurant like the ceiling over his bed. After his mother's death, it was his only competition for Papà's time. Stephano knew his father would want the business to go on. He walked into the kitchen to survey the remains of a lifetime—the giant ovens that swallowed sticky dough and spat out warm crusty pizzas and baguettes, the huge dishwashers that steamed up the entire area and the gleaming pasta presses perched on the counter near the back wall. Stephano was home. Now, he would test the sauces and taste the tiramisu. It was now his love—his responsibility. He went back and placed the urn on the counter next to the cash register.

The door rattled as Maria jiggled her key in the lock. Maria had been the bartender/hostess for over a decade. Maria knew almost as much about running the restaurant as he did. Benny 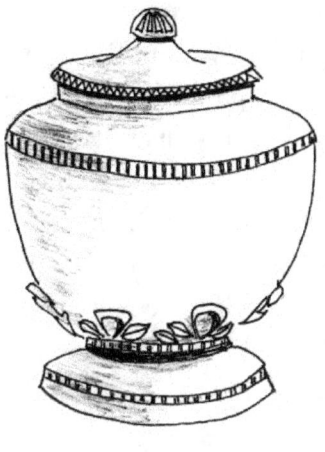 believed if he treated his employees like family, they would return in kind. Maria was never late and she never worried what time the last customer left. She was almost as dedicated to the business as Benny himself had been.

Maria was still in her black morning clothes from the service. Stephano was sure she should've taken the evening off.

"How are you my son?" she said as she entered the modest vestibule. Benito had believed any place people could not eat was a waste of space.

"Maria, what are you doing here?" Stephano said. "You should be home. Papà would have wanted it."

"Benito would be here himself if he could climb out of that urn."

"You're right; maybe I should tape the lid down?" Stephano said, a faint smile revealing itself.

"Maybe you should find someplace that he would've liked and liberate him."

"Papà liked it here," Stephano said. "Perhaps a spot in the corner?"

"It's not like we don't have enough dust already. Set it in the back. No one wants to see Benito like that—cooked to pieces. You should take him home."

Stephano moved the urn back to the kitchen. He would try to find a suitable place later. It was time to work. Franz, the dishwasher/prep cook, came in, giving his condolences before heading to the kitchen. Angela, who waited tables, looked dubiously at the urn and gave Stephano a pitying nod.

The evening crowd was subdued. Several customers who'd heard about Benito gave their condolences. For the most part, it was an average crowd on an average night, but without Benny's enthusiasm and his unique ability to make people feel good about eating the 1,300 calorie meals, something was missing. By one a.m., Stephano was ready to lock the door, flip the sign and head home. He wanted to leave his father there at the place he loved, but Maria had a point. No one wanted to see Benito reduced to such simplicity. He was a man who'd devoted himself to seeing people happy. He'd created a place where people could relax, relieve themselves of their worries, where he could welcome old friends, and make new ones. *He had such a way.*

When Stephano arrived home, the small house seemed desperately empty. His father had always come in after the restaurant closed. The two would sit at the small wooden table in the kitchen and relive the day's events over a bottle of wine. They would mull the red liquid in small glasses and discuss its potential with food. They would laugh about the way customers tried to pry the kitchen's secrets out of the servers. They would talk about Stephano's mother and how they missed her.

Stephano set the urn on the table without thinking and opened a bottle of *Vino da Tavola*. He settled on one of the chairs and poured two glasses. Papà had never been without stories. He'd emigrated from Italy as a child after the war. Italy's economy had been devastated; America offered opportunity. His family had owned several small parcels of land, which they sold for passage to America. Benito's memories of the olive harvest and bread making were what inspired him to bring the Italy of his homeland to his new country. He'd never regretted his parents' decision.

Stephano drained both glasses and eventually the entire bottle. He felt weary; the day had been long and emotional. He would find a place for the urn tomorrow after the reprieve of sleep.

142

The next morning, he eyed the urn during breakfast and still half expected his father to knock on the door while he ate. No, Benito Calabrese would not be knocking on his door. Papà was gone. Time and a bad heart had claimed him as their own. He would not open the restaurant, share a bottle of wine, worry about the staleness of the bread, or eat leftover Pasticotti for breakfast. Stephano found himself undeniably alone.

Why hadn't he married? Why didn't he have someone to scramble eggs for breakfast or rub his shoulders? Because, like Papà, his life was afternoons and evenings at the restaurant. When could he meet a wife? Only if she came in the kitchen and professed her love over rising pizza dough. The urn was going back to the restaurant. It was not a good breakfast companion.

Stephano investigated his slightly balding scalp as he shaved and brushed his teeth. He was not a bad-looking man for his age. But how many dates had he been on in the past decade? One a year, maybe? Women were not attracted to men who reeked of garlic and stunk of Gorgonzola. Women wanted men with barreled chests and fat wallets. He was an Italian doughboy who hit on waitresses and delivery women. His last date was for lunch. No one falls in love over salad and iced tea.

He looked at the urn as he headed out the door. Papà could have the restaurant.

That evening, the crowd had thickened and Papà's longtime customers were back, many of them with stories about Benito and his warm and gracious personality. Benny had bought a hundred raffle tickets at one time from a local charity. He delivered leftover food to the homeless kitchen. He had purchased advertising from every rag in town. Most of the customers were concerned about the future of the restaurant and who would be taking over for the garrulous Italian.

When Stephano opened his door late that evening and saw the urn still sitting on the table, he too began to remember stories. How he'd wanted to play basketball and how Papà had forbidden it. "I need you here at the restaurant," he'd said. "And how high can a short Italian kid jump anyway?" When Stephano had hoped to try out for the soccer team, Papà had said they couldn't afford it. There were the invitations to hang out with friends and drag Main St. in high school, but Stephano had to fill in for the prep cook or mop the floors. Somehow, Stephano became thirty-six, without children, without a wife, without even as much as a steady girlfriend. He'd never been on a vacation. He'd only seen a few movies that weren't matinees.

He'd never attended a concert or gone trick or treating as a kid. He could, however, select the best wine for any dish or find the season's finest oregano. He knew when pasta was cooked to perfection and the importance of freshness to a particular sauce. What he didn't know was how to start a conversation in a bar or book a hotel room. Or how to characterize a woman by what scent she wore or shop for lingerie. Stephano would not, could not, let Benito's Bistro become his mistress. There had to be a way to own a restaurant and have a life. Surely, his monk-like existence wasn't terminal. He could live outside of the kitchen. The urn belonged at the restaurant seven days a week. He did not.

He'd tried Internet dating. It had resulted in a lunch date with a sexy blonde who seemed to be unavailable in the middle of the day after that. He'd kept up a few other e-mail relationships for a while. The problem was, as Stephano saw it, most women didn't want go on a date at midnight or midday. Even the plainest girls had standards. He had to hire someone to manage the place at least part-time. Surely, Papà could understand that. Stephano couldn't be expected to do everything.

The next day, he called in a help wanted ad to the local paper and posted one online. He began getting calls and e-mails immediately. Many of the inquirees had never worked in restaurant management. Several of them only seemed concerned with medical benefits, hours, and the like. A few of them made appointments to be interviewed and never showed up. He decided to put up a sign in the window. Maybe no potential employees would see it, but perhaps customers would understand if their spaghetti was a little late.

"Stephano, no one wants to work this late," Maria said, as soon as she learned of the search. "You might as well be looking for a vampire."

"If the vampire is experienced in restaurant management, I'd say he has a job!"

On the third day, Stephano was surprised when the blonde from his lunch date entered the Bistro right after he had turned the sign. She was prettier than he'd remembered.

"Hi, how are you?" she said, recognizing him.

"Good, what can I do for you?" he responded, straining to remember her name.

"Do you remember me? I'm Ariana."

"Yes, Ariana, of course I remember you."

"Well, do you still need a manager?" She was smiling.

Oh yes, that smile. Would it be awkward if she worked for him? Could he come to terms with her rejection? What if handsome boyfriends or even a husband dropped in to see her now and then?

"We do. My father passed away not too long ago. I need someone who can help me manage and take maybe three of the night shifts."

"May I fill out an application? You know, I've been managing the restaurant at the Fairmont Inn and I have been working five evenings a week. I could live with three."

How could I not have recalled that? "I have an application right here and you're also welcome to leave a resume," he said, motioning to the paper in her hand.

"I'll bring you something this evening," she said, backing toward the door and still smiling.

Stephano waved. *I'll probably never see her again—as it should be.*

When Ariana dropped off her application and resume, Stephano was busy in the kitchen. He found the form completed neatly and thoroughly, lying next to the register.

"Pretty girl," Maria said, as he folded the application. "And smart too. She didn't bother you while you were in the kitchen."

"I'm thinking of hiring her for the assistant manager position."

"Good idea. Your Papà almost worked himself to death. You are much smarter," she said turning away.

The next morning, Stephano, looked at the application. He couldn't find any reason not to hire Ariana, except that she was far too attractive to be sweating over pizza ovens and baking lasagna. How difficult would it be to have her scent following him around on slow evenings? What if in a ridiculous flair of passion he touched her hair or placed his hand on her back?

So far, she was the only qualified candidate. The least he could do was to grant her an interview. After he'd unlocked the restaurant door and secured his jacket, he took out the paper and dialed the number. He was surprised that she picked up the phone on the first ring. Unprepared, he took a deep breath before speaking her name. "This is Stephano at Benito's Bistro. Would you be available for an interview today or tomorrow?"

"Of course. What time is good for you, Mr. Calabrese?"

The use of his formal name caught him short. "M-maybe at three o'clock?" he stammered.

"Perfect, I'll see you then."

He felt his face flush while he hung up the phone. She must think I am the biggest dolt on the coast. What if I offer her the job and she doesn't even accept it. Who would give a woman so many chances to reject them?

Ariana didn't refuse the job offer. She accepted it on the spot. Stephano was encouraged when she wanted to start training the next day. With any luck, he could be munching down a tub of overpriced popcorn in front of the big screen by the weekend.

But luck was not on his side. Maria came down with what she described as "consumption" and stayed home for an unprecedented three days. Stephano thought maybe it was *fortuna*. He and Ariana were able to complete a thorough inventory. They even sat down and shared a glass of wine after flipping the sign one night.

He liked her. She was smart, relaxed, and the staff seemed to be comfortable around her. In fact, work that week didn't seem much like work at all. He was certain that she would become what his father described as a *buon impiegato* or good employee.

It wasn't until two weeks later that Stephano began to notice a change in Ariana. He stopped in every evening to check on things and pick up the bank deposit. She'd begun to avoid his presence.

One night as he was leaving the storage room, Ariana was attempting to enter the small space. He'd switched the light off and before he could flip it on again, she'd stepped into his arms. He wasn't certain who made the overture—but for several seconds he found himself locked in an embrace with his new employee. The kiss had been sweet and passionate. Only the longing that resonated from his fingertips down to his feet equaled the shock he experienced afterward.

He didn't go to the restaurant the next night. Not knowing how to respond to the kiss, he figured the money could just wait until Ariana was off. He was relieved when he came in the next evening and found no trace of his new coworker. As the other employees filed in, he thought he might have seen a small glance in his direction. Did they know? Had someone walked past the storage room during his embrace? Was he the town goat boy and didn't realize it? The tension lasted until the last customer was ticketed, and he knew he was almost free from the suffocating suspicion. Just as Stephano was turning the sign around, Ariana opened the door. She smiled and surveyed the room with a cutting slant. "Can we talk?" she said.

"Sure. Have you eaten? Some bread maybe?" If he'd learned anything from Papà—it was that very few situations can't be improved with bread and wine.

They sat in the back. They discussed the night's receipts, the kitchen's limitations, the need for new menus and the poor quality of the season's tomatoes. Finally, Ariana looked him in the eye. "Stephano, why didn't you ever ask me to dinner?"

"I have always been here. Papà never wanted to turn his *amore* over to strangers."

"And look where it got him. He is still here watching over you!" she said, pointing to the urn, now perched on top of the wine cabinet.

"I didn't know what to do with him. It was strange having him at my home."

"The point is that you need to have a life that is more than Benito's Prison."

"I went to a movie Friday. It was very funny. I enjoyed myself immensely."

"Did you go by yourself?"

"Of course. Who would I take? Maria? Franz? Everyone is here."

"Take me." She looked down at the empty bread basket.

"If I take you, no one is watching the restaurant. Papà always said he was successful because of his passion. He was always here."

"Stephano! Close the restaurant one, two nights a week. Let's go do something." She was almost pleading, or maybe she was just angry. He was having a difficult time reading her.

"This place is my father. He is this place. I am not ready to leave his principles. He came to this country with nothing but a dream—to live some place where hard work paid off. I should be praising him for all he accomplished."

"Geez. I give up. Don't you want to love? Don't you need to have some fun? Can't life be about living?"

148

"Yes, yes. I know what you're saying is true. That's why I hired you. But the kiss, I wasn't expecting the kiss . . ."

"Stephano, I wasn't expecting it either." Her words hung like dust motes in a stale room. She grabbed her things and walked toward the door. "I'll be here at four tomorrow," she said over her shoulder. The door slammed in the darkness.

It wasn't meant to be. I am the son of a cucini. I am married to dough and garlic. Tomorrow I will apologize and accept my punishment.

He didn't want to go to the restaurant the next day, but staying away seemed cowardly. *A man does not avoid the inevitable.* He would wait until the evening rush and then he could be in and out without worrying about extended parley. Yes, that would work.

By the time the dinner crowd was echoing outside, Stephano had everything rehearsed in his head. A swift confession followed by an offer of conciliation. Maybe a few words about a proper working environment and he could out of there in fifteen minutes, twenty tops.

The mood was especially festive when he opened the door. The candlelight danced, sweet soothing smells rolled through the doorway. This was the Benito's of his childhood. He could see plates of lasagna carried by Angela and Ariana past a menu board that read: Special: Benito's Lasagna.

"Have some lasagna; it is especially delicious tonight," Maria said in his direction. So far, so good. He headed for the kitchen.

Ariana came back to the kitchen, smiling. *Ah, that smile.* How could he say no to such beauty?

"What's the secret ingredient?" Stephano said, hoping to appear at ease.

Just then, he looked across the kitchen and spied the urn sitting on the pasta counter. He walked toward it and saw the lid sitting on the counter. An accident? Had someone been cleaning the wine cabinet?

"Stephano, I'm so glad you came by. We're really busy. Could you help with the wine glasses?" Ariana, said.

"Certainly," he responded, walking toward the dishes. "Hey, I heard the lasagna is really good."

"Yes, my own special recipe," Ariana said, smiling, glancing across the room.

He followed her gaze back across the busy kitchen. It had settled on Benito's urn.

The Roadmaster

Wagon Wheel, Texas (1952). I asked her to come with me to the car dealership. Breitling, the old man who lives across the street, said to me, "Elmer, when you gonna buy your wife a new car?" None of your gottamn business, I wanted to tell him. The S.O.B. has nothing better to do than sit in his back yard and shoot squirrels out of trees. It really isn't any of his business, but in this small town—only 20,000—everything is everyone's business and if that asshole Breitling thinks I'm a tight wad, everyone else probably does too. So, I'm goin' to get the money out of the bank, buy local and give 'em all somethin' to gossip about.

~~~

He asked me to go with him to the car dealership, which I found odd. Normally, when he has a notion to purchase a new vehicle, I don't even know it. He just leaves in one car and comes home in another. He's never consulted me before. It's a man thing. Even though I owned a car before I met him, he sold it right after we married; part of a life I gave up to become Mrs. Elmer Edwards.

My papa owned the local ice company located on the edge of town. Then, ice was delivered to people's houses. Papa was a good man. Everyone liked him. He died when I was in my thirties. We think he had cancer. But back then, people just died. I heard people say that my mama was the prettiest woman in the county. She was also a good seamstress—kept three girls in nice dresses. I

151

started to sew by hand when I was about four. By then my older sister had taken over a lot of the sewing and I wanted to be just like her. It was around the end of the war when Papa bought Mama a treadle machine. I couldn't wait to get my hands on it.

Mama was also a good cook—had to be—she never knew when Papa was going to bring someone home to supper. Since there was already six of us—"what's one more?" he used to say. People watched out for each other. When someone got sick, we took over food. When someone died, we helped bury them. If we had extra food in our garden, we shared.

~~~

I was the only boy and the youngest. I barely remember my mother. She died when I was four. "Probably pneumonia," said the doctor who arrived from town hours afterward. I had three sisters. The one closest to me in age was decent—treated me right, unless the other two got hold of her. My oldest two sisters were a couple of hellions. They'd make fudge and hide it from me. Never bothered to call me to the table to eat. Never gave a gottamn about anyone except themselves. Daddy was usually off workin' and expected them to watch after me, but they never did unless I was botherin' them. Daddy would give 'em money to buy me school clothes and they'd spend it on somthin' stupid. Neither of 'em had a lick of sense.

~~~

When Elmer came to town he had a beautiful car. Nicer than anything I'd ever seen. He stayed with his aunt one summer to work in the fields. She was an old maid who'd inherited some land from her parents. My sister went out with Elmer once and vowed, "Never again." But I thought he was smart, and he was willing to work for a living, which a lot of fellas weren't. He only had an eighth grade education, like a lot of folks then, but Elmer had dreams. He'd heard about a new way of showing pictures. They moved on a screen and he was planning to start a motion picture house in California. It sounded a lot more exciting to me than teaching school out in the country. He wanted to travel and I had only been to the city a couple of times. It was a pretty easy decision. Besides he was one of the few boys I hadn't grown up with and already knew like a brother.

~~~

She's a pretty lucky cook, probably the best in the county, least that's what I tell her—lucky—not good, which sticks in her craw a little, but keeps her from getting too high and mighty. Mildred's fried chicken, mashed potatoes and smooth cream gravy was the best I'd ever had. She could sew and knew how to can and freeze. She'd also gone to college and was pretty smart for a gal in those days.

I have always been the breadwinner, handled the money and the financial decisions. Important things need not include womenfolk. I give her money when she needs it. Her part-time job at the store keeps her from asking me for much, which is how I like it. Otherwise, women will soak you dry. Never met one that wouldn't take your last dollar.

~~~

We usually shop for groceries together, not cars. Elmer compares prices, tells me what we can afford and when we get home, he methodically ticks off each item on the tape and checks the total.

It must work though, we've never lost a home or a car and we survived the great depression when half the country was lined up at government-run soup kitchens at one time or another. He wanted to go; after all, it was a free meal. I, however, refused because we had food—plenty of food. I gardened every summer, freezing and canning enough fruits and vegetables to last for years to come.

Once when we were first married and he was out of town, I lived on cornflakes for days—never again. I thought I had plenty of food and ran out before I could make it into town and was too embarrassed to ask for help.

~~~

Mildred and Elmer arose early on the morning he wanted to go car hunting. She cooked a breakfast of eggs, bacon, and biscuits. Next to ice cream with peanut butter, biscuits were Elmer's favorite. She used to roll out the dough and cut her own, but the canned ones were much faster. It had taken her months to convince him to spend the extra money. Finally, she simply told him that if he wanted homemade biscuits on the mornings she had to work, he would have to make them himself.

He was ready before seven a.m. and she was certain the car dealership was not open until much later. He always wore his oldest clothes when he shopped. Convinced that any price quoted to him was based on what he looked like he could pay.

"If you dress like royalty," he would say, "they'll expect a king's ransom." He had worn a pair of pants that he had bought in the '20s, shoes with holes, a starched shirt with frayed cuffs, and a brimmed straw hat trimmed with a nasty black sweat stain around the band.

She, on the other hand, took her time to tease her hair and select a dress for which she had matching shoes and a purse. He took one look at her when she emerged from the bedroom and sent her back to change. She reluctantly put on a dark paisley dress given to her by her sister. Ill-fitting and not her color, it was nothing she would have ever chosen for herself. Again, he sent her back to change. *What does he want me to wear—rags?* Eventually, she chose a house dress, a duster. *I should just wear my slippers too. No, canvas shoes. That'll show him, I'll wear my gardening shoes.* She was embarrassed to be seen in public, but he assured her she wouldn't see anyone she knew. This didn't make her feel any better.

They left at seven-thirty a.m. and "appearing a little too anxious," she told herself. Dark was fleeting when they arrived. They parked near the entrance and waited. When small promises of light began to emerge, he pulled into the lot and headed for the back area.

"Why are we parking back here?" she asked, facing a plate-flat dusty field on the edge of town.

"I don't want them to see our trade-in right away," he said.

Trade-in? she thought. *You call this a trade-in?* She pondered further.... *This hulking piece of Detroit after-birth would be better off being sold by the pound as scrap.* Words she could never say aloud, and what did she know anyway? This was a man's world.

After hiding the car, they strolled up to the showroom and began pacing the front lot looking at the shiny new behemoths and sorting past them one by one. He was drawn to the blue ones. Blue was his favorite color. She hated it. He'd bought a blue wheelbarrow and blue shirts; he had wanted to paint the house trim blue, but she had stopped him by buying her own paint and painting the trim a nice plain white while he was gone. He had not complained. It was the sort of work he despised.

They walked the entire lot, passing by several cars that she liked the look of. He quickly dismissed each one with comments about price, model, or motors, which she knew nothing about. She readily got the idea that he had been here before. This was confirmed when a salesman with oily hair approached them and called her husband by name. Elmer introduced her and the salesman said he was sorry she'd been ill and was pleased to finally meet her. She had not been ill since the swine-flu epidemic of 1949. She simply shook her head, partly in embarrassment, partly because she didn't know what else to do.

"That blue Chevy you were looking at has been moved inside," the salesman said. "So many people have been interested in it, my boss decided to clean and polish it up."

155

"We'll just keep looking around out here. My wife doesn't know what she wants yet," the old man responded.

So he brought me here for sympathy! He has no interest in what she wants to drive. She had been schlepped along as a bartering dupe. Well, she was not going to be seen around town in a blue car. It was simply not her. No matter how new or how shiny.

They finally went into the showroom to look at the car. It wasn't just blue; it was the bluest of blues. She had never seen anything so ugly in her whole life. Even the interior was blue. She looked at the price—not great, but reasonable compared to the other cars. It *was* priced to sell. A hundred less and it was a done deal. She stared in disbelief. She would rather hitch up a team of mules like her mother had done than drive this bright blue albatross.

"Now, how much do you want for this one?" Elmer asked, ignoring the figure on the windshield.

"We could probably take fifty off of this," the salesman responded, pointing to the invoice.

"That's still quite a bit," Elmer said.

"Well, I don't have a lot of say in pricing; they come to us already priced. That's Detroit's doing. What year is your trade-in?" he asked.

At that very moment she became sick to her stomach. This deal was happening whether she liked it or not. Something in her snapped. "It's a '41," she volunteered. The two men glared at her, as if she had suddenly grown two heads and a tail. "We bought the Coupe at Ford's year-end sale." Ignoring raised eyebrows, she explained that even though it had 50K miles on the odometer, it still ran beautifully as long as you slowed down before applying the brakes. Good, she thought, I have their attention. The men studied one another.

"Could we please drive one of the beige Buicks, the one on the end?" she said a few moments later, pointing out the window.

"Sure, I'll g-get the key," the surprised salesman said, looking to her husband for approval that was not forthcoming.

"What the hell are you doing?" her husband cursed when the salesmen walked off.

"I want to drive that car. It has a large backseat and a curved windshield."

"It's too expensive. That gottamn car is probably at least five hundred more than this one. Buicks are always overpriced."

"Hush, here he comes!" she said.

The salesman stood there not knowing to whom he should hand the key. The old man made an abrupt move toward the salesman that was probably meant to intimidate him, but the clueless salesman just dropped the key on his palm. They walked across the lot alone. He muttered obscenities under his breath and she felt good enough to skip. He got in the car, immediately raising his voice and began complaining about the angle of the seat and the ignition location. He started the car with some difficulty and backed out of the parking place. "These gottamn Hydra-Matic transmissions are nothing but trouble. We'll never get a good deal on a car if you keep 'em thinking we can afford the most expensive car in the county."

"We can afford it," she said.

"You aren't paying for it. When was the last time I saw any of your money?"

"This morning at breakfast, when I fixed your eggs, you saw some of it then." He was silent, angry, and didn't know what to say.

"Rides nice, don't you think? We could use it on vacations to visit Mary and Arthur."

"I'm tellin' you, it's too gottamn expensive!" Now he was shouting.

"Pull over, I want to drive."

He hit the brakes, pitching her forward. She got out in the weedy ditch and made her way around the car. She opened his door, listened to his cursing, and waited. He eventually got out, raising his voice even more, continuing the rant as he climbed into the passenger side. She was grateful no one could hear him. She had never driven an automatic transmission before. But she wanted to drive, so she shifted to where the indicator pointed to "drive." They took off smoothly and she was able to veer back onto the road with no problems. The car rode like a dream. It steered easily; she could see out of the windows better than any other car she had ever driven. The seat was comfortable and the car effused class. It was a lady's car. She had driven trucks, tractors, and even a Harvester combine once on the farm. But this was a *ride*.

When had her opinion stopped counting? She had worked as hard as he had. She had taken every bit as much responsibility for their finances. Maybe she didn't go to the bank, but she shopped for used clothes she could alter or refashion for herself and the kids. She had hung out the laundry by hand whenever weather permitted saving a trip to the laundromat. She cooked three meals a day from scratch. They never ate out. She had endured the aggravation of slip covers, flat sheets made from flour sacks and government cheese longer than anyone she knew. She ground her own meat, packed lunches for hired hands, and gave her own perms. By God, she counted.

When they arrived back at the car lot, she felt like royalty whose carriage was slowed by deft coachmen in knee pants—the fantasy quickly dissipated by the old man's cussing. When they got out he was still grumbling, said he was going to the car and stalked off. With key in hand, she walked in the direction of the showroom only to meet up with the salesman before she was halfway there.

"How was the car? Where did your husband go?" he said without giving her a chance to answer.

"He wasn't feeling well; said he needed to rest."

"I'm sorry. Can I get him something? We have sodas inside."

You can get him a shot of whisky, because after this—he'll need it. "How much is that Buick?"

He quoted a number that was, as predicted, significantly higher than the blue Chevrolet. "Let's sit down. I do want to learn more about the Roadmaster—I believe that's what it's called."

And learn she did…she used every automobile phrase she had ever heard. What is the car's horsepower? Does it have a four-barrel carburetor? What is power steering? So, what is a fireball engine? Is this straight-eight engine hard to work on? Is it reliable?

She asked so many questions that the poor salesman got one of the mechanics for back-up. They eventually had to refer to a service manual for some of the answers and even mentioned calling Detroit at one point. After this had gone on for several hours, she suddenly rose from the seat she had felt permanently affixed to.

"Thank you so much for explaining all of this to me. You know all the women in my Sunday school group have been talking about getting new cars. They are such a competitive bunch. I know that if I get this car, after they see it, everyone will want one. Then I'll have to see myself comin' down the road. Just like the time Mary Beth Collins and I bought the same dress from the JC Penney catalog. Neither one of us could wear it. Maybe I should shop at a dealership further away."

The salesman's face took on a determined look. "Well, we might be able to get this car in a special-ordered color. I could make some calls. Some dealerships do that."

"Oh, really? Is that possible?" she sunk back down on the chair.

She could see the animated salesman back in the main office. Time after time he hung up the phone. She could feel her legs going numb. She should ask if there was a ladies room. *No. That would be a sign of weakness.*

Finally, he came out with perspiration beading on his forehead like a detective in a summer heat crime novel and a smile

159

on his face. "I found one in Cartersville that is a beautiful silver-blue called Nassau blue."

Damn. I should have known. They're all color-blind. "Silver, you say?"

"Yes ma'am."

"And how much is this car?" she asked. He responded after checking his notes.

"That is really more than I have to spend right now and I really don't know about silver."

"That's before your trade -in though."

"Oh, about my trade-in, it's the brown Ford parked in the back. But there's a boy up my street that has his eye on my car. I've known him before he could walk. His daddy says he will give me way more than anyone else, 'cause he knows me and knows how good a care we have taken of the car. I'll have to talk to him before I can do anything. But thank you so much for all of your help." Again she rose from the chair, suppressing the need to urinate.

"Ma'am, let me talk to my boss, he really makes these decisions."

"Okay, that's fine. I'll just go to the ladies' room and freshen up if you'll point me in the right direction."

After she returned, she sat back down on the chair that was starting to remind her of the principal's office when she was a schoolgirl. She had to stand. Her body was past relaxing. Maybe she should check on her husband. He could have left without her. As she stood once again, the salesman returned. "He says he can come down to the price of the blue Chevy." She thought a minute. "And how much for my trade-in?" The bewildered salesman left shaking his head. Ten minutes later he returned with the amount for the trade-in. "I better go now. I need to check on my husband. When could you have the car here?" she said, as an afterthought.

"In a couple of hours."

"So, if I come back in two hours with cash, we have a deal?"

"We really need the financial arrangements worked out before we bring the car over."

"Well, let me speak to my husband first," she said, trudging toward the door, leaving the flustered sweaty salesman again.

Once in the parking lot, she realized that not only had she committed the "cleave unto your husband" sin, but that he was never going to give her the money. She opened the passenger door to find him snoring in the driver's seat. After one of his rants, he always napped like a fat tabby on an August afternoon. She eased gingerly into the seat. Looking over at his tilted portrait, she was reminded that her husband was both predictable and impulsive. He planned for success, but his rants were uncontrollable. He had planned to buy a car today, and he had the money for a car in his pocket—

She took a long, shallow breath. She could see the outline of his billfold through the old, saggy britches and reached toward the pocket. With a single motion she had the leather billfold in her hand. She carefully opened the glove compartment and found the Ford's signed title. Quietly, she slipped out. Once outside, she counted the bills in the wallet. There was more than enough for her car even with tax. She took out the money, closed the billfold and shoved both of them into her purse.

As she returned to the showroom, she could see the salesman in the back on the phone. It had been a mistake. She had returned too soon. She should have waited at least a half hour before coming back in. She turned to leave. He dropped the phone and began walking in her direction.

"I spoke with my husband and he still thinks the price is high for us. Could you drop the sales tax?" she spit the words like discarded watermelon seeds.

"The salesman stared back in disbelief. I don't think so. I would have to speak to my manager."

"I understand, dear. Never mind. I told my husband you probably couldn't do that."

"Well, I can ask him. I just don't think it is possible."

"Okay, son, if you don't mind."

Again she waited. Her hands were warm, her hip was bothering her and she would not sit in the uncomfortable chair again. Another ten minutes ticked by. She headed toward the door. The fun was gone. She wagered on a losing hand. Odds were better at church Bingo. She was tired. Suddenly, she heard the click-clack of the salesman's shoes.

"He says we can split the sales tax with you," the salesman said, nearing her.

"That sounds like a something we can do. Where do I pay?"

Once again, the surprised salesman guided her to the office. He turned her over to a young woman who began shuffling papers. The salesman walked back to where the phones were. An older woman came in, counted the money into piles on the desk while the younger one clicked away on an adding machine. "Your car should be here about the time you have all the papers signed," she said.

The woman had never bought anything that required her signature. There were waivers, disclosures, a bill of sale and a warranty agreement. She had never seen so many legal documents.

Eventually, the papers were signed. The salesman returned with the key and handed her an envelope. They walked out to the lot where she eyed the most stylish car she had ever seen. It was the color of her husband's eyes; light and clear with a hint of blue. It reminded her of the young, ambitious man she married. It was so pristine she could see her reflection on the door panel. She walked around it. It looked like a spaceship that could deliver her to a new planet or a distant galaxy. It was without blemish, fresh with possibilities. None of the weariness of her life was visible in the shiny, metallic paint. Its newness intrigued her. It was the first important financial decision she had even made on her own; completely on her own.

"Let me get my husband," she said to the relieved salesman. "Can I drive it? It's mine now, right?"

"Sure it's yours. I just need the key to your Ford."

For a fleeting second, she thought about retrieving the key and leaving her sleeping husband there in the car on the lot. "I'll just leave the key in the other car, okay?"

Climbing in the driver's seat, she realized that she was meant to have this car, blue color and all. It felt just right. She could drive this car from here to eternity. It fit. She pulled up beside her sleeping husband and honked twice. He raised his head and glared. She rolled the window down. "Hop in, we are going to try this one out," she shouted.

To her surprise, he opened the door of the new car and got in. *Gottamn.*

According to Wikipedia, Roadmaster sales dropped in 1952. Sales in 1951 were 66,000 cars. In 1952, sales were down to 51,000, probably accounting for the discounted price.

Sheli Ellsworth

If you like to laugh, you will enjoy Sheli's first book, *The Psychoanalysis of Everyday Life: Sometimes I Pee When I Laugh*. Her second book, *Confessions of a Pet Au Pair: the ABCs of Pet Ailments,* written with co-author, Bill Wafer, DVM is a fun, informative work of creative nonfiction. Her book, *My Winter Holiday by Noah,* is an interactive picture book for children ages 4-8 written with co-author Sheldon Brown and illustrated by George Robertson. Sheli is also the illustrator of a children's picture book, *Henry the Helicopter*, written by her husband.

www.ingramcontent.com/pod-product-compliance
Lightning Source LLC
Chambersburg PA
CBHW070035260626
47159CB00005B/2049